Tales of the Were
Redstone Clan

Matt

BIANCA D'ARC

This book is a work of fiction. The names, characters, places, and incidents are products of the writer's imagination or have been used fictitiously and are not to be construed as real. Any resemblance to persons, living or dead, actual events, locale or organizations is entirely coincidental.

No part of this book may be used or reproduced in any manner whatsoever without written permission, except in the case of brief quotations embodied in critical articles and reviews.

DEDICATION

With many thanks to the fans who keep me doing what I do. And to my family, for sticking by me through thick and thin.

I particularly want to thank Peggy McChesney and Jessica Jarman, for their help in making Matt the best it can be. Special thanks to Valerie Tibbs for creating the perfect cover for this story.

And to my Dad, who is a trooper beyond compare. Though he'll never read any of my romance stories, his support in my personal life has been invaluable as I make my way in this crazy world we all live in. I love you, Dad.

CHAPTER ONE

"This is bullshit," Matt groused as he pushed his way out the door of the county's land development office, already late for another important meeting.

Grif, head of the Redstone Construction empire and Matt's eldest brother, had sent him to Northern California to straighten things out. So far, the mess only seemed to be growing. Grif was going to be pissed if Matt couldn't get a handle on the situation soon. This deal was big and had the potential of creating goodwill between shifters and vampires that might spread to other parts of the country.

In addition to being the CEO of Redstone Construction and Matt's brother, Grif was also Alpha of their family, and the Clan, as a whole. The Redstone Clan was one of the largest and most influential in the United States, with Redstone Construction—and every shifter who worked for them—at its heart.

The Clan had started with their extended family of cougar shifters. As the business grew, the Clan had welcomed many other shifters indigenous to the Americas, including many wolves, a few bears, raptors of all kinds, and others. There was the occasional drifter of one species or another that sought membership in the Clan, as well as work at one of the many construction projects Redstone Construction was involved in, at any given time, all over the U.S. and Canada.

Right now, the problem spot was Northern California, as it had been for some time while they tried to get this project off the ground. As youngest of the founding family and the only unmated brother of the ruling family, Matt had been sent to unravel the tangle of red tape, legal bullshit and crooked politicians. They also sent Matt because he had a few very influential friends in Northern California, including the client, Atticus Maxwell.

Atticus was a world-renowned vintner. He also happened to be a centuries-old vampire. But for all that, he wasn't a bad guy. In fact, Matt counted him as a close friend, which was odd, considering the usual friction between vamps and *weres*.

Redstone Construction had been hired to build a housing development for the Maxwell Winery's new shifter workers. Hiring shapeshifters was something new, and from all accounts, it appeared to be working out very well for all parties.

The ancient vampire had employed humans to manage his vineyards for years—centuries, probably. This foray into hiring a few select *were* families was something Atticus had been working on for a while now with the help and blessing of the Master Vampire of the region, a fellow named Marc LaTour.

The idea was to increase the connections between the Brotherhood of vampires and the *were* community. It was an initiative the Redstones endorsed, mostly because Matt had recommended this particular nest of vampires highly…and vouched for them personally.

There were a lot of family members of those who worked for Redstone Construction and had become affiliated with the Redstone Clan that didn't work directly in construction. Some, it turned out, were ideally suited for work at a winery. After a trial period, Maxwell had been so pleased with the results that he'd extended their contracts and hired Redstone Construction to build housing to suit the needs of the newest Maxwell Winery workers.

The land they'd chosen had an abandoned gold mine on it, which was perfect for the mostly wolf shifters who would live there. The old mine would provide a modicum of freedom and safety for the werewolves who liked the idea of raising their cubs in a place that had all the human creature comforts of a home above ground, as well as all the earthy peacefulness of an honest-to-goodness den.

But the mine that made the land so attractive in the first place was also the source of the current political trouble. Some eco fools had taken it into their heads that Redstone Construction posed some kind of danger to the environment. And, if that argument didn't halt construction on the site, the claim that Redstone Construction was somehow going to unleash chemical hazards that were leftover from the mine's active phase was also being bandied about.

Add to that media attention that neither the shifters nor the vamps wanted and the politicians taking fatuous stands on the manufactured *issue*, it could quickly become a business nightmare of epic proportions.

The land use people had been throwing around legal terms that made Matt want to strangle someone. Luckily, Maxwell had promised help from someone who knew the local laws. Regardless, Matt called his brother on the way to his next meeting with Maxwell's legal guy.

"Sorry, Grif. This is turning into a bigger tangle than we expected." Matt talked to his eldest brother via cell phone as he maneuvered his truck down the winding road that led to the Maxwell winery.

"I'll send Louise from Legal up to you. Maybe she can help," Grif offered. "She can probably be there by tomorrow."

"Atticus promised me one of his guys. I'm going to meet with him now. Atticus wants this project built as much as we do. He says this year's vintage is going to be the best in centuries because of the delicate noses of his new werewolf employees. Apparently, they can smell exactly when the grapes are at the peak of ripeness or something."

Grif chuckled. "Glad to hear they're getting along."

"Getting along? You have no idea. Atticus was practically gushing about the new vintages. The dude was in alt. He thinks they've got a lock on some kind of prestigious prize that pretty much guarantees he's going to make another fortune. He's talking about profit sharing, since he credits his new staff with the leap forward they made this year."

"That's really good," Grif answered, smug pleasure in his tone. "Those wolves needed something better suited to their skills than working in a construction office. I knew Jenny and her siblings were wasted here."

Grif was a really good Alpha. Matt knew his brother had checked on Jenny Fesan and her family many times throughout the experiment. He cared that they were not only well treated, but happy with their new jobs.

"Yeah, no doubt," Matt answered, switching the call from the hands-free tech in his truck to the handset as he parked the vehicle outside the winery's business office. "The land use guys gave me the runaround, but hopefully, Atticus's lawyer can help me untangle the mess. Hold off on sending Louise until after I talk to Atticus's guy, okay? Chances are, Atticus has got enough clout up here that their guy can get a lot further than our people would."

"All right. I'll alert Louise but hold off on sending her up there until I hear back from you. Call me back after you meet with the local lawyer."

"Will do, bro. I'm heading into the meeting, right now. Call you in an hour."

They hung up and, Matt opened the door to the business office, his eyes adjusting from the bright sunlight outside to the dim interior. Atticus wouldn't be at the meeting, Matt knew. He was a vampire, after all. He and his mate wouldn't rise until the sun went down, but that was okay. Atticus had left instructions for his staff, and they were used to that kind of thing.

Matt walked up to the reception desk and gave the human woman sitting behind it a broad smile. Matt liked women.

Young, old, tall, short, and everything in between, it didn't matter. If they were female—and nice—he liked them. He didn't go in for mean girls or women with bad attitudes, but if they had a good heart and kindness in their soul, it didn't matter what they looked like on the outside, he liked them.

The plump older lady behind the desk smiled back, responding to Matt's greeting.

"You're Mr. Redstone, aren't you?" she asked. "The big boss left me a message to expect you. He set up a meeting for you with our legal counsel." The older woman stood and bustled around the desk, inviting Matt to follow her. "Everything's all set. I took the liberty of providing refreshments. If there's anything you need, please just buzz me, okay? My name is Irma."

Irma opened a door and motioned him through. He paused on his way in to take his leave of the receptionist.

"Lovely to meet you, Irma," Matt replied, smiling back at her. She seemed to have a perpetual grin on her face.

She left, closing the door behind herself, and Matt turned to look over the big conference room. It was more of a library, actually. The far wall was lined with floor-to-ceiling bookcases that held what looked like a complete set of state law books. Oh, yeah. He was definitely in the legal department.

A movement to the right by an open window caught his attention at the exact same moment a breeze wafted the most delicious scent toward him. A scent he had caught only once before but had never quite forgotten...

"Morgan?" Matt turned to find the loveliest woman he'd ever met looking at him with a crooked smile on her face.

It had been more than a year since he'd seen her, but the encounter was still fresh in his mind. She had made an impression on him. A lasting impression.

"Good to see you again, Mr. Redstone." Her voice was low and mysterious. Just as he remembered.

"Call me Matt," he answered automatically, smiling at her simply because he was happy to see her again.

He'd spent more than a year thinking about her, which was odd, but not unexpected. She was, after all, the only Florida panther shifter he'd ever met. They were a related species to his own cougar, but slightly smaller and indigenous to a different part of the country.

"I suddenly remember you're a lawyer. I thought you worked for Marc LaTour, though," Matt said conversationally, moving toward her.

"I've worked for most of the Brotherhood at one time or another, actually," she said casually, even as her spine straightened at his approach.

He made her nervous, but she was standing her ground. *Brave little kitty.* Matt's inner cougar liked that about her.

"You look as lovely as ever, Morgan," Matt observed, stopping just a bit in front of her. He gave her room while still allowing himself to bask in her delicious scent. His cat wanted to rub up against her and lick her skin to see if she tasted as good as she smelled. *Down, tiger.*

"Thank you," she replied to his compliment, a bit of color highlighting her cheekbones as she beat a strategic retreat to the side, edging around the conference room's large center table. "Would you like some coffee?"

He followed her to the sideboard that had been laid with a wide assortment of refreshments, just as Irma had promised. Matt helped himself to a bag of cheese puffs while Morgan poured coffee for them both at his nod.

She turned to the table and took a seat near a small mountain of papers, several open law books and a laptop that was already open and humming. Matt noted the wire that ran from it to the center of the table where an audio-visual hookup was located. Morgan put down her coffee and picked up a remote as he took a seat in the chair a few feet down from hers.

Morgan pointed the remote, and the window shade lowered, blocking the sun while she dimmed the lights. A screen rolled down out of the ceiling on the other end of the room and another button made her laptop's display show on the screen.

It showed a map Matt was quickly becoming very well acquainted with. It was the old gold mine with an overlay of the proposed housing development.

"This is the plan we gave the county," she explained unnecessarily. "I know you have other plans that we can't show the humans, but from what I've discovered about the county's concerns, if we can find a way to doctor these plans—the ones we submit to the human authority—and provide a way for the human inspector to see exactly what is on the revised plan and nothing of what you're really doing, then we might be able to pull this off."

She proceeded to point out the problem areas and asked astute questions about modifications that could help. She suggested a ruse of blocking off the old mine completely to satisfy the human land use office, while secretly constructing a new entrance the werewolves could use.

"There are a few points the county is concerned with. This is the biggest one." She gestured toward the display. "They don't like the idea of even the small usage of the old tunnels that you disclosed on your plans. They don't seem to want anyone in the old mine, at all," Morgan went on.

"We've done these kinds of projects before, all over California," Matt said, thinking through the problem. "In past projects, we found it eased the human inspectors' minds if we acknowledged the old shafts and showed that we knew about the risks, shored up the areas that were easily accessible, and made sure nobody got any farther into the old mines than our plans showed." He munched on a cheese puff and thought some more about the strange situation they found themselves in here. "In the early projects, when we made no mention of using the old shafts, at all, that's when we had problems. As soon as we altered our approach, this went a lot easier. The guys here aren't behaving normally."

"Should we worry?" Morgan turned to him in the darkened room, her eyes narrowing in concern.

It was on the tip of his tongue to tell her to leave

everything to him. His instinct was to protect her, but that wasn't giving her enough credit. Plus, if she worked with him on this, he could spend more time with her.

"We can fix the plans to show what they want," he said instead. "What I'm more worried about, frankly, is the threat of eco protestors and media attention. We're going to need to find a way to nip that in the bud."

"Atticus left some thoughts about that," she said, consulting some of the papers at her side, then turning to her laptop to go to another image. "This topographical map shows the boundaries of the land Atticus bought for this project. This parcel..." She pointed to an adjacent section that sat over the deepest part of the old mine. "It's up for sale. Atticus suggested we look at the possibility of turning it into a nature preserve to pacify the eco warriors. It might also prove a nice place for your people to utilize for hunting and running around. Atticus asked only that you tell them not to bite the tourists."

She smiled at the small joke, and Matt was enchanted. He almost forgot to breathe there for a moment.

Totally uncool, fool, he mentally chastised himself. Matt got a grip and tried to concentrate on the matter at hand.

"That shouldn't be a problem. Jenny and her family have had all their shots," he quipped back, proud that he had saved himself from looking stupid, drooling over the pretty lady. "I'll talk to our designers. We should be able to get something together quickly both on the revisions to the building plans and the nature preserve. I'll have them work straight through the night on this, if we have to. I want to avert any sort of media attention."

"I agree. In fact, if this gets out of hand, Atticus is prepared to scrap the project. The last thing he—or your people—need is too much media attention. I'm sorry to have to say that, but those are my instructions, and frankly, I agree with his decision." She at least looked sorry, even if such a decision would mean the shifter employees would have to keep living in uncomfortable human housing.

Oh, the houses they currently occupied were luxurious by human standards, but shifters had different needs. Privacy, for one. They needed room to roam, and female wolves, in particular, liked to have a den to retreat to once in a while. The mine's tunnels would've been perfect for a growing werewolf population, and now, with the addition of a nature preserve nearby, the place would be perfect for shifters. Matt resolved to make this work.

He just had to preempt any protests and get new plans approved in time for the groundbreaking ceremony that had been rather optimistically scheduled for next week. No way did he want to cancel that. He had his work crews already on the way here to start work. The last thing he wanted was a costly delay—or worse, a cancellation of the entire project.

Morgan cleared her throat when he didn't reply. "For now, though, let's proceed as if we're going ahead with the project. In which case..." She clicked over to a new drawing. "Atticus had some questions about this tunnel here." She pointed to the portion of the old mine that ran very close to the vineyard.

They discussed some modifications Atticus had proposed, and Matt made notes. He decided as they went along that he'd draw up the new plans himself. It would be easier for him to do it on-site than have to explain all the changes to someone at Redstone Construction's home base in Las Vegas. Plus, the things Atticus wanted to add were both brilliant and demanded the utmost secrecy. Matt didn't want to trust the various data-transmission technologies with this. He would do these himself and keep it off the cloud, just to be safe.

Plus, it would give him an excuse to hang around. Atticus had extended an invitation to use one of his empty offices while Matt was there. Knowing Morgan was in this building made him want to stick around. He could manufacture a reason or two to talk to her during the day and maybe convince her to share a meal with him, if he played it right.

By the time she'd run through the rest of her images, Matt

knew exactly what he would do to alter the existing plans—both the publicly filed version and the *real* version. He also had a plan for luring the lovely Morgan to have dinner with him. Now all he had to do was get cracking on the plans so he'd be free in time to romance the lady over a candlelit dinner. Maybe with a bottle of Maxwell's finest...

Oh yeah, Matt had big plans.

Morgan was barely holding it together. She'd thought her memories of the youngest Redstone brother were somehow overblown. No way could he really be that handsome, or attractive, or downright sexy.

Then, he'd walked into the conference room, and her stomach had clenched in reaction. *Damn.* He really was all those things. All those things and more.

The man ought to come with a warning label.

Morgan did her best to maintain her professional demeanor through the meeting, and she finally hit her stride when they started to really work through the proposed changes. She found out then that Matt was as quick-witted as he was good-looking. His sharp mind impressed her, and his dry sense of humor tickled her funny bone.

Everything about him was appealing. *Dammit.*

She couldn't afford a distraction like him. Not now. Possibly not ever. Morgan had a plan for her life, and it certainly didn't include getting involved with a silver-tongued devil. Silver, after all, was poison to magical creatures like her.

Morgan was a professional woman. A career woman. No way did she want to become a shifter's mate, sentenced to nesting and making a home for her cubs and not using her brain and qualifications to work. Morgan had worked hard to become a lawyer. She loved her job and the people she worked with. She didn't want to lose the life she had carefully crafted for herself after the loss of her family.

Marc LaTour, the Master vampire of the area, had taken her under his wing. He'd paid for her schooling and given her a job. More than that, he'd given her a reason for living after the deep depression of losing everyone and everything she had ever known had almost killed her. Marc had been there for her, and she loved him like a father—or maybe a much older brother—for all that he had done for her.

She didn't want to give up all of that to become a shifter's mate. She had seen the way the women in her own family had been subjugated by the men. She remembered the fact that no woman of her Clan had been allowed to work outside the home. Women were supposed to stay home and raise cubs, according to the old Alpha of the Clan in which she had been raised until her teen years.

And she saw the same thing in the werewolf women who now worked for Atticus. Although Morgan hadn't talked to them, she knew from the building plans that they were nesting—making homes for their young. Morgan wondered how many of the female workers would keep on working for Atticus once the new houses were built. In all likelihood, they wouldn't. Atticus was going to be saddled with a werewolf community in his territory, in which only the single women and the males worked.

She had counseled against building permanent housing for the shifters, but Atticus had done it, anyway. It was his land, after all. He would be around long after Morgan and this current generation of shifters was gone, so the problem would be his for a long time to come, if it turned out the way she expected. It was his decision, and she was only here to follow his orders.

Keeping those thoughts firmly in mind, Morgan was able to hold back a bit of her inner cat's response to the cougar sitting so close. Matt was an imposing man, and his cat was probably even more impressive, but Morgan was going to be cautious. She would work with the man, but that was as far as it could go.

Decision made as their meeting came to an end, Morgan used the intercom to ask Irma to set up a vacant office for their visitor. The older lady would make sure Matt had everything he needed, and Morgan might be able to make an escape. She needed breathing room—preferably in a place where every inhalation didn't bring more of Matt's deliciously masculine scent into her lungs.

"We have one of those big printers that can do engineering drawings," Morgan mentioned as she collected her papers. "Atticus likes techie stuff, and he doesn't spare any expense when it comes to the latest office equipment. We use it to print up marketing materials, signs, posters and the like, but it'll do large-format drawings, too."

"That sounds just about perfect," Matt said, though the look in his eyes when she met his gaze made her think he was talking about more than just a printer.

* * *

Matt worked on the drawings all afternoon as far as Morgan could see. She couldn't help but be curious about his comings and goings. She saw him walk past her office door a few times on the way to where the large-format printer was kept. Each time he returned from the printer, he had another giant sheet of paper with schematics on it in his hands.

He was using the empty office a few doors down from her own, and she could hear him move around, as well as the clicking of his computer keyboard and mouse. Shifter hearing was sharp, and the rest of the office was pretty quiet. Plus, she was interested in the man, despite her better judgment, and couldn't seem to help but track his movements.

He moved very quietly. He was a cat, after all. But she was able to hear the mechanical noises of the equipment he used. The scratch of his pencil against paper. The rustle of the large-scale drawings as he moved them around. The click of the clip that held his cell phone to his belt as he removed it and made a call.

She could even hear his side of the conversation that followed. It was pretty clear he was reporting to his brother, the Alpha of the Redstone Clan. Matt had offered Morgan the protection of that Clan when he'd first met her and realized she was unaffiliated with a Tribe, Pack or Clan of any kind. She was a loner and had been since losing her family.

Although...she had been taken in by the Brotherhood. She could never be one of them, but they watched out for her, all the same. There were no romantic entanglements. She had never been interested in any of the bloodletters that way. For one thing, she had been very young when she'd been orphaned and pretty much adopted by the vampires. For another, she had spent a lot of time away at school, which the Brotherhood had paid for. When she returned, she went straight to work for them. The only men she had been involved with in a romantic way had been human boys at school, and they couldn't keep up with her for long.

She hadn't met many shifters in her life. Just the few who had dealings with the Brotherhood. Although, that was becoming more common as the Master and his right-hand man, Atticus, seemed intent on strengthening the relationship between their enclave and the Redstone Clan; though, they also had friendly dealings with the Lords of all North American *were*.

That was something new. For centuries, or so Marc had told her, the Brotherhood had stayed far, far away from shifters. He'd also told her that they'd worked together in ancient times to defeat and banish the fey woman known as the Destroyer of Worlds. But, after that threat had been dealt with, for some reason, the former allies grew farther and farther apart.

"Got a minute?" Morgan looked up to see Matt leaning in her doorway. The man moved silently, but his yummy scent now wafted through the room, making her inner kitty sit up and purr.

Down, girl. She had to work with the man. She wasn't interested in how good he smelled or how handsome he looked. *Right?*

"Sure," she said, putting aside the paperwork she hadn't really been able to concentrate on, anyway. "What's up?"

"I've got a good start on what we talked about, but there

are a few points I'd like to discuss with you before I go any further." He walked into her office, bringing the drawings with him.

She stood and met him halfway. There was no place to lay out the big sheets of paper in her workspace, but there was a table just down the hall that would work.

"Follow me," she invited. "We can lay this out in the break room and snag a cup of coffee while we're at it."

He reversed and allowed her to precede him out of the small office. She felt him following close behind, the papers in his hands waving out behind him like a flag. The image it made in her mind brought a little grin to her lips. For such a masculine guy, Matt Redstone hadn't really impressed her as the office nerd type, yet he was proving he could push a pencil with the best of them, if need be.

The lights in the break room came on automatically as they entered, and Morgan went directly to the coffee station while Matt laid out his poster-sized sheets of paper on the table. She fixed a cup for herself, then turned to offer Matt a cup, which he declined.

Putting the cream back in the small fridge, she went over to the table, sipping her light, sweet coffee. She looked at the new schematics, noting the box on the lower corner that held the name of the person who drew them up. Her eyebrows rose as she saw Matt's name in there, bold as daylight.

"I didn't realize you were doing these yourself. I thought you had teams of architects and engineers back at your base who handled this stuff."

"We do," he agreed. "I help out from time to time. In addition to being one of the owners of Redstone Construction, I'm also a fully licensed civil engineer, which is what we need for these particular changes. I've been working on this project since its inception because of my friendship with Atticus. We all want this alliance to succeed." Matt shrugged, easing his stance a little. "Plus, it's just easier for me to revise the plans here, rather than send them back and forth. More secure. And faster."

She was impressed but didn't say anything further on the subject. They set to work, and Morgan realized Matt had a few very astute questions and suggestions on how to make the changes. He added a few details to the nature trail in the newly-proposed preserve that would allow humans to use the area without letting them get too close to the truly wild areas they wanted to keep private for the *weres*.

She liked what he'd come up with and was able to answer most of his questions about the specific laws of the county and state without having to refer to her books. There was one nitpicky question about setbacks from the property line that she had to double check, but aside from that, they spent a very productive twenty minutes discussing the changes he'd already made and the ones he would work on that afternoon.

"I want to get these done tonight," he said as he rolled up the plans. "Can I convince you to join me for dinner? I know more questions will arise as I finalize everything. It would be helpful to have your input, so we can file these with the planning guys tomorrow morning."

Was he asking her out? His phrasing was vague enough that she could take it either way. Either he was simply a colleague who wanted her to stick around for his own work-related reasons, or—and this was the option that gave her the heebeegeebees—he was asking her out because he was attracted to her and figured work was a handy excuse to get what he wanted.

She watched him carefully, trying to figure out which it was.

"Come on, Morgan," he said playfully. "Give a guy a break. You're looking at me like I have ulterior motives."

"Do you?" she came right out and asked, one eyebrow raised in challenge.

Matt transferred the rolled plans to one hand and moved closer to where she stood, empty coffee cup in hand. He held her gaze, and she suddenly realized her breathing had grown faster. Not good. She wasn't prey. Never would be. She was just as much predator as the bigger cougar. It was time he understood that.

"Maybe." Matt seemed to read her expression and backed off a bit. She hadn't been ready for that reaction, and it took her a moment to process his lighthearted smile as he leaned one hip against the table, watching her. "But you can't blame a guy for trying, right? I promise, if you join me for dinner, it'll be strictly business. I really do want to get these drawings done tonight, so there's no more delay on the project."

She thought about it. He seemed sincere. And mischievous. But, then, he was a cat, after all. Cats were known for mischief. She ought to know. Her own inner cat got her into trouble often enough that she was familiar with the phenomenon.

Curiosity was another trait she had trouble with, sometimes. For example, right now, her curiosity was pushing her to find out just what Matt Redstone had in mind. Would he be the polite businessman at dinner? Or would his wildcat come out to play?

She simply had to find out.

"Okay. A working dinner. Here," she stipulated. "I'll order in. There's a place we use regularly. Atticus does a lot of soirees and dinner meetings and always provides food for his guests. Do you like salmon?"

"Fish, beef, fowl," he agreed. "Anything in the carnivore range." He smiled, showing his pearly whites. "Although a little lettuce, now and again, is good for the digestion, I hear." He gave her a mocking, doubtful expression. "Order anything you like. I'm easy." He winked and headed for the door.

"I'll just bet you are," she murmured, knowing he would hear. His chuckle as he went back into the office he'd been given was downright sinful.

CHAPTER TWO

Matt worked straight through the afternoon, pausing only occasionally to call and confer with the architectural team back at Redstone Construction's headquarters. He spoke to Grif briefly, assuring the Clan's Alpha that he had things under control.

He worked on the show plan—the one they would file with the human government. The secret plan was also adjusted slightly but remained on Matt's secure laptop, in a highly encrypted file. He had just printed out the final draft he wanted to go over with Morgan when the aromas of dinner came down the hallway toward his borrowed office.

His stomach started rumbling, reminding him that he'd pretty much skipped right over lunch. A few snacks, here and there, pilfered from the break room didn't make much of a meal for a hungry shifter.

He rolled the plans and followed his nose to the big conference room where Morgan was unpacking a series of insulated bags. Dinner had arrived, it seemed, and from the gourmet scents tickling his nose, she hadn't spared any expense.

"Smells delicious," Matt said, walking in and heading straight for the sideboard where she'd laid out the plates and utensils.

"I ordered a little extra, since I figured you'd be hungry," she said, still working on laying out all the different platters and sauces.

Shifters ate a lot, burning off any excess in the process of shapeshifting and running in their beast forms. Morgan knew this, being a cat shifter herself, but to any human looking at the spread, it probably seemed like she'd ordered dinner for eight. At least.

Something else struck him. Her words and actions hinted at the fact that she was aware he hadn't eaten lunch. Matt's inner cougar growled in satisfaction. She'd noticed him. While it wasn't a huge step forward, it was still a step. She'd cared enough to notice he hadn't eaten and had made sure to order extra food so he could eat his fill. She cared at least that much about his welfare, which was a start.

"Looks good." Matt sniffed as he leaned over her shoulder, eyeing the food. The scent of fine cooking was making him salivate, but Morgan's scent set his senses on fire—as she had done since the moment he'd met her.

"Wait 'til you try the salmon. I don't know how they do it, but their recipe is one of the best I've ever tasted." She enthused as she unwrapped two healthy portions of the pink fish. She dumped a whole fish on her plate, giving him about the same amount when he held his plate out.

He'd start with the fish, since she seemed so taken with it. Cats liked fish. Of course, cougars liked just about any meat, preferably raw. But Matt's human side could appreciate the flavors both cooking and sauces brought out.

He added a few more items to his plate and sat with Morgan at the big conference table. His drawings were rolled up on the other end of the table, to avoid getting soiled. Matt was hungry enough to push aside work for the moment.

They ate in comfortable silence for a bit, Matt trying each of the dishes Morgan had ordered. She had good taste. And the caterer was top notch.

"This is all delicious," he commented after he'd tried a little bit of everything. "But you're right about the salmon.

I've never had better."

She smiled in agreement, toasting him with her fork, which was loaded with another bite of the creamy pink fish. She washed it down with some of the purified water they used in the winery and stocked in the office in plastic bottles.

"Luigi knows how to cook," she said after delicately wiping her lips with a napkin. Matt never thought he'd be jealous of a thin piece of paper, but there it was. *He* wanted to touch her lips—preferably with his own. "He's our go-to caterer, and he never fails to impress the clients."

Matt needed a change of subject as he studiously looked at his half-full plate. He was already planning on seconds. Maybe thirds. But he didn't want Morgan to see how attracted he was to her. Not just yet. She was skittish and had to be approached from the side. A head-on attack would only scare her off.

"So, you've told me how much Atticus likes his new employees and their superior sniffers, but what about you? Have you had time to meet Jenny and her family? I know they're wolves, but there don't seem to be a lot of other shifters around here for you to socialize with. Have you made friends, yet?"

She took a moment before answering, her voice subdued when she finally spoke. "I've never really had any friends like me. Not since my family was killed. The only Others I know now are vampires, and they've treated me well. I remember how it was in my Clan, and I don't really want to go back to that—or watch others suffer in that kind of environment."

Matt grew concerned. "Was there something wrong in your Clan?"

"Probably not in your eyes." Her voice turned bitter.

"What's that supposed to mean?" He was getting really alarmed now. Was her Clan abusive? Was that why she'd avoided her own people? It wasn't common, but it had been known to happen from time to time.

"Well, you're a man. Men rule in the shifter world. Women sit home and have babies. And speak when they're spoken to," she said, all in a rush. "I prefer Marc's idea of a woman's place. In school. In the office. Equal intellectually, even if we're not always equal in brute strength."

"Whoa… Hold the phone. You really think that all shifters keep their women barefoot and pregnant?" That might explain a lot about her attitude, but how was he to overcome such thoughts?

"Well, don't they? I haven't met a single woman who works for your company. So far, it's all guys. And Jenny and her family are all single, unmated women. I know they're nesting. Once you build those homes with the nice, comfy dens, I anticipate Atticus is going to lose most of his new workers to maternity leaves that never end."

"Oh, man…" Matt tried to interject, but it seemed Morgan was on a roll.

"I tried to tell Atticus this, but he doesn't believe me, for some reason. He told me to wait and see, but he doesn't understand that once he lets these wolves into his domain, he's going to be stuck with them."

"Whoa, there." Matt held up both hands, palms outward.

He didn't quite know where to start with refuting her beliefs, but he had to set the record straight. This was his Clan she was talking about. They weren't Neanderthals. Women held positions of power in the Clan, but apparently, Morgan hadn't seen enough of the Clan to know any better.

"I suppose you're going to try to tell me that your Clan is different. That the men don't rule. That your Alpha is enlightened." The sarcasm in her tone almost made Matt's rising anger get the better of him, but he held it together.

"My Alpha—my brother—*is* enlightened. We're not cave men. We don't keep the women at home. They do as they please, and if they want to work for the company, they are given jobs to suit their abilities. You haven't met any of them, yet, because you've been dealing mostly with the construction team leader to this point. The design staff is almost seventy percent female. Many of them mated. And our legal team is headed up by a female raptor who makes most of us shake in our boots. The woman is formidable."

Morgan looked like she didn't believe him. Damn. The woman was stubborn.

"Look, if you won't believe me, then maybe you should talk with our priestess. Kate will set you straight." He tried to be understanding, but Morgan's doubt struck him through the heart. "I don't know what you saw in your home Clan, but most shifters don't live like that, anymore. There might've been a time in the past when we did—just like humans subjugated their females, and still do in some parts of the world—but Redstone isn't like that. My mother wouldn't have stood for it." He had to smile, remembering his brilliant mother. "She was a research scientist, you know. Kept working in her laboratory until the day she died. She raised us all to respect women and made sure every male in the Clan did the same. She was our Matriarch in the truest sense of the word."

When Morgan didn't say anything, he looked up at her. He knew there was a brightness to his eyes that she wouldn't miss. It happened whenever he thought of his mother.

"I heard she was murdered," Morgan said softly, her words bringing it all back in a flash. The pain of losing the woman who had been at the center of his young life. The pain of seeing his baby sister suffer the loss. The pain of knowing there was nothing he could do but avenge her death by finding the ones responsible.

"We caught the bastards who killed her. Her spirit was given justice. But nothing can bring her back. We all still miss her. Every day."

Morgan's soft hand covered his on the table, surprising him. "I know the pain of loss. I'm sorry."

And then, he realized what she must have gone through. She'd lost her entire family at a young age. She hadn't had a Clan left to go back to, but somehow, Marc LaTour had found her and helped her. He'd taken her under his wing and paid for her schooling, encouraging her to do whatever she wanted with her life.

Matt shifted his hand under hers, turning it up and interlacing their fingers. "That goes both ways. Marc told me a little bit about your background, and I'm sorry for what you went through." He let that sink in a bit before he went on. "But things really are different in my Clan. In most Clans, Tribes and Packs nowadays—though, there are a few throwbacks." She pulled her hand away, and he let her go. "At least let me try to prove it to you."

She eyed him suspiciously. "All right, I'll bite. How? Are you going to parade a bunch of your women in front of me to tell me I'm wrong?"

Matt sat back in his chair, looking at her. "I could do that, but I think you need to hear it from the women you unknowingly insulted. Just how much do you really know about Jenny and her family?"

She returned his appraising look. "Jenny is the ostensive leader of her family here. She's single. The girls are relatives. I don't know the relation, exactly, but they're all unmated. I'm assuming that's why you let them come here to work."

"Let?" Matt scoffed, truly amused. "There was no *letting* about it. Jenny wanted something new, and it was her decision to come." His voice lowered. "She's a widow, Morgan." He saw the surprise, quickly veiled, on her face. "Her mate died in an attack linked to everything that happened last year. There's been some unrest in Las Vegas. We tried to keep it quiet, but there was a vampire uprising…" He trailed off, waiting for her to indicate whether or not she'd heard about it.

"Marc briefed me after it happened. A guy named Raintree tried to unseat the Las Vegas Master, Antoinne de Latourette. Apparently, the plot was foiled by a female bloodletter named Miranda van Allyn." She recited the facts coldly, and she apparently didn't have the whole story.

"Miranda is quite a woman. A business owner. An educated woman. And my brother's mate."

"What?" Morgan looked truly shocked. "But that's forbidden."

Matt tilted his head. "Not really, as it turns out. It's not common, but there are a few vampire-shifter couples now. Some of the bloodletters, if they're old enough to have fought Elspeth the last time, say there were such matings back then. The theory is that they'll be needed if it comes to all-out war with the *Venifucus* again."

He named the ancient group who once supported the fey sorceress, Elspeth, known as the Destroyer of Worlds. The organization had survived the centuries with one goal in mind—freeing Elspeth from the prison of the farthest realms to which she had been banished so long ago.

"We're still keeping it as quiet as we can, but most of our Clan knows, as do most of the bloodletters left in Las Vegas. Master Antoinne—we call him Tony, when he's in a good mood—came out and declared himself on the side of Light, and made every bloodletter in his domain swear fealty to the Lady and Her Light, or leave. The few that didn't want to cooperate were hunted down and staked by Tony himself. It's been a rough few months back at home." Matt ran a hand through his hair. "The reason I'm telling you all of this is so that you know how Jenny's mate, Ray, died. He helped us fight and paid the ultimate price for his support."

"I'm sorry. I didn't know." Morgan's voice was subdued.

"The four younger girls with Jenny are her daughters. The two older women are her sisters. And you're right. They're all unmated. Ellie and Jemma, Jenny's younger sisters, owned a coffee shop, which they gave to Jenny's son, Robert, and his mate, Jilly, as a wedding present while they joined Jenny in her new start, hoping to support their older sister through this time of grief. I'm not sure if you realize how it is with wolves. Often, when one mate dies, the other follows. But we're doing everything we can to keep Jenny here with us, for her children and the rest of her family. She is well-loved and respected. She was a gourmet chef. Trained in Paris. She worked for one of the big hotels on the Las Vegas Strip, serving their high-rolling clients while her mate was a construction foreman for one of our wolf Pack teams. They were a core pair in their Pack and losing Ray was a blow not only to his wolf Pack, but to our Clan as a whole. We love Jenny, and we will protect her and support her as best we can. She wanted to leave Las Vegas, and it was her idea to volunteer for this project when I mentioned her situation to Atticus."

"He didn't tell me any of this," Morgan admitted, blushing slightly. "I'm sorry. I really am."

"Don't be. Atticus kept it quiet out of respect for Jenny's situation, but I think you need to know that not all Clans are like the one you came from. Talk to Jenny and her family. I think they'll tell you what Clan life is really like." Matt leaned forward. "We're not meant to roam alone all the time, Morgan, even if we are cats. We need the company and care of others like ourselves, from time to time. My offer still stands. The Redstone Clan would welcome you if you ever wanted to cease your loner ways." He smiled to soften his words and stood, breaking the somber mood that had descended as he told Jenny's sad story. "But, for right now, I'm going for another piece of that delicious salmon."

He refilled his plate, spooning up some for Morgan when she eventually joined him. They ate the second helping in near silence as she seemed to be digesting his words, as well. He was going for thirds when the phone in the center of the conference table rang. Morgan leaned forward, hitting the speaker button.

"I saw the light on and figured you were working late again, Morgan," Atticus said by way of greeting. His voice sounded the tiniest bit chastising—as if he found Morgan working late a lot and was used to teasing her about the long hours she kept.

It was just after dark, and the vampire and his mate had risen for the day. Their home was deeper into the vineyard, but though they couldn't quite see the house from the business office, the office was visible from the house's yard. No doubt Atticus had simply gone outside and spotted the lights in the office from his backyard.

"Matt and I were sharing dinner and just about to go over the changes he made to the plans today," Morgan replied.

"Changes? Yes, I saw your email. Since you're still here, why don't you come down to the house? I'd like to see the new plans. Say, in a half hour?" It was more order than invitation, but Matt didn't mind. He counted Atticus as a friend, even if he had been born in an entirely different century.

"We'll be there," Matt answered after Morgan nodded.

With a few more pleasantries, they rang off and began cleaning up the remains of dinner. There wasn't much left, and Matt wasn't shy about eating any crumbs left in the serving dishes. Before long, they were ready to roll.

Matt tucked the plans under one arm and headed outside with Morgan. It was a lovely night, the crisp, clear air of the Napa Valley illuminated only by starlight now that they'd locked up the office for the evening. Matt had his laptop in its soft case looped over one shoulder and Morgan had her pocketbook.

"It's not far," she said, looking up at the sky. "We could walk, if you don't mind. I've been cooped up inside all day, and it's nice to be outdoors."

Matt knew that feeling. His inner cougar didn't necessarily like being stuck inside all day, either. What he really would have liked was a nice, long run in his fur, but since that wasn't on the agenda at the moment, a short walk in the starlight would do nicely. He'd have to hoof it back up here to get his car later, but he didn't mind. Especially if he managed to walk back with the lovely Morgan. Her car was up here at the office, too, after all.

They walked down the gravel driveway that led to the main house. Not many people were invited to the vampire's lair, but since Atticus and his mate, Lissa, did a lot of socializing and had to drive one of their many cars, the driveway was a necessity. Matt wasn't fooled by the lack of any obvious surveillance equipment. The bloodletters were notoriously private and protective of their homes. Matt had no doubt they were being watched by robotic eyes every step of the way down the path toward the European-style villa at the heart of the vineyard.

"It sure is pretty here," Matt said, opening the conversation. They were both cats with excellent night vision. There was no excuse to hold her hand or touch her in any way, much to his disappointment. "Do you get out to run much?"

"Not as much as I'd like, but occasionally, I prowl the vineyard with Atticus's blessing. He says it keeps the mice down, but I think he just says that to tweak me." She chuckled, and he could see the small grin on her lovely face in the starlight.

"I have no doubt of that. Since he found his One, Atticus has been full of laughter. It's a good change for him. Marc, too. And, especially, Sebastian." Matt named the three bloodletters he was closest with from the Brotherhood that had congregated in the Napa Valley. "I'm happy for them."

"I have to agree. Mating has been good for them, though it certainly hasn't mellowed them. If anything, they're hyper-vigilant now."

"They have to be," Matt agreed. "They have mates to protect. Nothing is more precious than a mate. Especially when you've waited so long to find her." He cleared his throat, knowing he'd sounded a little too wistful there, for a moment. "I see it with my brothers. All four of them have found their true mates now. They'll do anything to protect their ladies and vice versa. The mate bond is a special, rare thing."

"You said one of your new sisters-in-law is a bloodletter. What about the others?"

Matt liked the very real interest in Morgan's voice.

"They're all pretty formidable. Grif's mate, Lindsey, was born human, but her grandfather was a Native American shaman. It's a complicated story, but in some kind of shamanistic ceremony, the Goddess's Light turned Lindsey into a cougar. Grif had to teach her how to shift, how to be a cat…everything. But she's doing amazingly well. She's a strong Alpha female and is slowly learning to fill the Matriarch role in our Clan." He paused, thinking of his mother again. But he couldn't dwell on the sadness. That would get him nowhere. "Steve's lady is pretty incredible, too. Trisha has some amazing magic over water. Her father, it seems, is descended from a water sprite. You know about Miranda, Mag's mate. And then, Bob found a lady bobcat shifter who is kind of adorable when she's in her fur. That little stubby tail and her furry ears are cute. We're taking bets on what kind of cubs they'll have, when they get around to it."

"So, only two of your brothers mated shifters?" She seemed interested, which Matt counted as a good thing. At least he had her questioning. Maybe thinking about what she'd seen as a youngster versus what he was telling her about his family. "Is the Clan okay with that?"

Matt shrugged. "Our Clan is kind of huge and encompasses many different breeds of shifters within it. They're pretty accepting. We've all learned how to cooperate and get along over the years. And, universally, shifters respect power and those who wield it for the good of the Clan. My new sisters-in-law have proven themselves over and over again. They are true mates to my brothers, but more than that, the care and love they show my brothers extends to the Clan. None of them had an easy road to mating. They each faced threats of one kind or another. Some of those threats also threatened the Clan as a whole, but they didn't back down. These ladies wielded whatever power they had for the good of the Clan and to protect their mates, as my brothers did the same. Everyone in the Clan can respect that. So what if Trisha is part mermaid? And accepting Miranda is easy when you see her and Mag together. It's so freaking obvious they were meant for each other, it's kind of disgusting." He made a comical face that earned him a chuckle as Morgan punched him lightly in the shoulder.

He liked the easy camaraderie they'd developed over the

past few hours. It seemed so natural to talk to her and laugh with her. Matt suspected there was a bit of being *made for each other* going on here, as well, but only time would tell. First, he had to get closer to Morgan. Close enough for him to know for certain whether or not what he suspected was true.

He wouldn't leave California this time until he knew, once and for all, whether or not Morgan was his true mate.

CHAPTER THREE

Morgan wasn't totally convinced that Matt's Clan was all he claimed it was, but she was at least beginning to think maybe she should give him the benefit of the doubt. She had stayed far, far away from shifters since her youth, preferring to go it alone.

She liked Marc and his friends. They had taken her in when she had no one else to turn to. They'd become her family in a strange, undead sort of way.

But, more than once, she felt the call of the wild that Marc couldn't fully understand. Vamps and weres were both highly magical, but they were different in a lot of respects. Marc and his friends would watch over her when she felt the need to run in her beast form, but they never could quite understand that other part of her. The beast part.

Just as she could never quite understand their bloodlust. She knew it for a real thing that had to be ruthlessly controlled, but she also didn't fully understand it. And never would. That's just the way things were, and she had come to a sort of peace with it. The bloodletters accepted her differences, just as she accepted theirs.

But Matt Redstone was like her. More so than any other shifter she'd met since being orphaned. He was a big cat. Moreover, he was a closely related species. A cougar to her

Florida panther. The bloodlines had separated hundreds of years ago with the panthers adapting to a small part of Florida.

Their cat forms were slightly smaller than the cougar that roamed in most of the rest of the country. Her breed was very localized and isolated. By choice. Her people had chosen to limit their contact with Others long ago and retreated to the backwaters of a small territory they defended to the last man. They'd become a bit inbred, she believed privately, which might explain why they were so backward and overprotective of the females.

She assumed there were others, still in Florida, but she'd been swept away in the night when her immediate family was killed. She'd been so young. She realized now that anything might've happened, but the Goddess surely had been watching over her when Marc LaTour found her. She'd told him her story, compelled by the magic of his voice. She'd been so young. She hadn't understood the power of the vampire, back then. All she knew was that her whole family had been savagely murdered, and Marc had convinced her to trust him with her tale of woe.

It turned out to be the best thing that had ever happened to her. He'd taken her in that night and directed his human servants to see to her needs. He'd paid for her care and made sure she was enrolled in school. He'd encouraged her to do anything she wanted to do, and when the time had come, he had paid for her ivy league education and even her law school tuition.

He was her savior, and her friend. Their relationship was comfortable for them both, and she was more loyal to him than to anyone else she had ever known—up to and including her old Alpha, who was, mercifully, long dead now.

Matt didn't seem anything like the Alpha males she remembered. Oh, he was definitely an Alpha. Her cat recognized the dominance of his nature right off. But he was...kind. There was a core of compassion in him that impressed her greatly...and confused the heck out of her, as well.

They neared the house in silence as she thought through everything he had told her. If he was to be believed, she had quite a few things wrong about the shifter world. Morgan didn't like to think she'd been close-minded, but Matt had given her much to ponder. She resolved to look into his claims, at the earliest opportunity, and she knew just where to start. She was going to have a chat with the werewolf woman, Jenny.

He'd been telling her about his family, but it was all too much to take in. She didn't know how to respond to his claims. She had to do a little more research first before she could believe him. Until then, it was just better to remain silent.

And the silence stretched… But the night was calm and the stars twinkled down on them as they walked companionably along the gravel drive. Before too much longer, Morgan was saved from her contemplation by the opening of the mansion door. Atticus had seen them and was coming out to greet them.

And by *greet*, she really meant *look them over before allowing them anywhere near his mate*. Atticus took protectiveness to new heights now that he was mated to Lissa.

He was wise to be cautious, though. Lissa had been human until meeting Atticus. He'd had centuries to perfect his defenses and skills while she was a mere fledgling in a world of predators. She would need a lot more time as an immortal before she could really handle her power with the same level of skill Atticus had attained over the many years of his existence.

Atticus surprised Morgan by taking Matt into a manly, back-pounding embrace. As if he was some sort of long-lost friend. Morgan had known they were close, but this was the first time she'd really seen them together in a non-business setting. She hadn't quite realized how deep their friendship really went.

"Good to see you again, Matt," Atticus said. "I hope the

locals haven't been giving you too much trouble."

"Nah. It's all good, my friend. Morgan has been a great help in getting the new design sorted out. I think this one will do the trick." Matt held up the rolled plans in one hand. "We addressed all their issues, and with any luck, we should be back on track once these puppies are filed."

"When do you plan to refile?" Atticus asked, casually ushering them into his home.

"First thing tomorrow morning, if you approve of what I've done," Matt replied diplomatically. The housing might be intended for shifters, but it was Atticus's land and money paying for it. He had final veto on any plans.

"Excellent. Let's take a look, shall we?" Atticus had led them into the living room and gestured for Matt to unfurl the plans on the wide coffee table in front of the couch.

Miranda took a seat off to one side, leaving the couch for the men. She needed a little space from Matt, right now. He disturbed her equilibrium just by existing. She wasn't quite sure what that meant, but it definitely gave her something to think about.

Matt pointed out the changes he'd made to the public plans, and Morgan put in her bit when called upon. Then, Matt pulled out his laptop and showed Atticus the secret plans. Morgan was impressed. She hadn't thought even Atticus would be let in on all the shifter secrets, but Matt was completely open with the vampire, as far as she could see.

"I like this nature preserve idea," Atticus said, sitting back. "It provides even more of a buffer zone between our people—and my home, too—and the humans. My mate's friend, Sally, could be of great help with the plantings. I think, with a little effort, we can create natural pathways that any human won't be able to thwart. There are certain prickly plants and vines that could be convinced to grow in deliberate patterns—in addition to what you've already thought of here, Matt. Sally has a way with such things, and she's mated to a wolf, now, so she can probably be prevailed upon to help make a secure home for Jenny and the other were ladies."

"Really? What Pack is she affiliated with?" Matt asked.

"Do you know Jason Moore?" Atticus asked with a shrewd expression.

"Jesse's brother? Alpha of the Wyoming wolf Pack?"

Even Morgan knew about Jesse Moore. War veteran and former Special Forces major, Jesse Moore had retired to a mountaintop in Wyoming, leaving the running of his home Pack to his younger brother, Jason. But Jesse's Alpha tendencies wouldn't be denied, and over the years, a mixed Pack of ex-soldiers had congregated around the werewolf. They had formed a mercenary unit that could be hired if the cause was just and the price was right. And they were all shifters of one kind or another.

Matt shook his head. "I'd heard Jason found his mate, but I had no idea the lady was connected with your Lissa."

At that moment, Lissa walked into the room, a smile on her face. "Forgive me for eavesdropping, but yes, Sally is one of my oldest and dearest friends. I'm sure she'd come help us if she can get away."

Lissa walked over to Morgan and gave her a quick kiss on the cheek in greeting. Then, she went to Matt, who had stood, and hugged him, too, which surprised Morgan. Atticus didn't let just anyone get close to Lissa. It was yet another indicator of the depth of Atticus's friendship with Matt.

When she stepped away, she headed for the sideboard that was laden with glasses. Morgan knew a wine cooler was located inside the antique cabinet, stocked with all of Atticus's favorite vintages.

"Can I offer you wine? Or other refreshments?" Lissa asked graciously.

Morgan accepted, needing a bit of fortification. Alcohol didn't affect shifters as strongly as humans, but a little wine might just help soothe her frazzled nerves. As Lissa handed Morgan a glass, they all heard a car coming down the drive. The motor had a deep-throated hum that spoke of an expensive, high-performance engine.

"Ah…" Atticus stood, heading for the doorway. "That's probably Marc and Kelly. Sebastian and Christy are on their way, as well."

That was news to Morgan. Seemed the Brotherhood was having a party.

"Marc, of course, wants to see the plans for the nature preserve, since it means more mortals in the area. But I think he'll like the way you've designed it, Matt. With a few tweaks in the forest, we'll have complete control over where the mortals roam. And when Sebastian heard you were in town, he wanted to come by and say hello. Hope you don't mind."

"Mind? Not at all," Matt answered jovially. Seemed the cougar was looking forward to being surrounded by bloodletters—which was not the reaction Morgan had expected, at all. "I've been meaning to visit them but have been too busy with this project before now. Once the plans are accepted by the human authority, then we can get down to the regular schedule of construction and there'll be more time for socializing."

Atticus nodded and left the living room to greet his guests. A few moments later, Marc LaTour and his mate, Kelly, arrived. Kelly went straight to Lissa, greeting her with a hug. The two were old friends from college and both had only been recently turned by their vampire mates.

Matt was respectful of Marc, as was only right when greeting a Master. Marc may not be the oldest vampire in the area, but he was the strongest and best suited to the role of Master. For that matter, Atticus could have been Master, but he didn't want the job, leaving it for his slightly younger, and very formidable, friend.

Since Marc had found Kelly, he'd been a different man. Once solemn and, sometimes, cold, Morgan had seen the real personality Marc must've had when he was mortal come to the fore. Kelly had brought that out in him. She had brought him happiness—and a reason to carry on. For that alone, Kelly was someone Morgan would lay down her life for. No questions asked.

Marc may have adopted Morgan, but she had adopted him, as well. He was her family—her father figure, her older brother. And all his friends were her extended family. Uncles, sisters and cousins, so to speak.

She knew it was odd for a shifter to be so close to a nest of vampires in this day and age, but they had taken her in and cared for her when nobody else had. They'd never asked anything in return. None of them had ever—not even once—asked for a hit of her powerful shifter blood. She knew there were no ulterior motives behind Marc's adoption of her. He simply had done it out of the goodness of his heart. He was her true friend. As were his extended family of vampires, and now, their mates.

Kelly and Lissa sat near Morgan, paying only scant attention to Matt and the guys as they went over the plans again. Morgan had come to respect the ladies after initially being wary of them. The addition of mates had changed the dynamic of their little family, and at first, Morgan had feared the change. But it had turned out better than she ever would have expected. The women had added a spirit of joy to the Brotherhood that had been missing for a very long time indeed.

Now, she considered the new mates friends. Even sisters. So, Morgan wasn't all that surprised when Kelly started looking from Morgan to Matt and back again, a mischievous expression on her face.

"So, what gives with you and the hunk?" Lissa finally asked in as quiet a voice as she could manage. Morgan cringed. Matt could probably still hear the question.

"Nothing, Lissa. Just working together, that's all," Morgan ground out, hoping Matt was distracted enough by his conversation with the guys that he wasn't paying attention to the ladies.

"But he's like you. A cat, I mean. Christy says he turns into a mountain lion," Kelly whispered.

It struck Morgan oddly, for a moment, that Christy would know more about Matt than the other women, but, then,

Matt was said to be closest with Sebastian, Christy's mate. He'd met Sebastian first, and then, Sebastian had introduced him to the rest of the Brotherhood, and they had come to be friends with him, as well.

"The Redstones are cougar shifters," Morgan confirmed, trying not to let any of her interest show.

"Oh, come off it." Lissa nudged Morgan with her elbow. "He's gorgeous. And a shifter. You should totally jump his bones." The last was said with a giggle that seemed to attract Matt's attention. He looked up from the plans and sent Morgan a smile coupled with a knowing wink.

He had heard everything the women said. She just knew it.

Morgan nearly sputtered, looking for something to say, but she was saved from having to answer by the arrival of Christy and Sebastian. Atticus let them in, and the couple went straight to Matt, greeting him with hugs and smiles. Lissa got up to pour wine for everyone, and the gathering soon took on a festive air.

At that point, the ladies got involved in the discussion about the nature trails and what their friend, Sally, could do to help coax the plants in the right direction. It was quickly decided that they should get Sally and her mate to come out to Napa once the trails were laid, so she could work her magic on the forest.

"Sally is part dryad," Christy announced, taking Morgan by surprise. She hadn't realized any of the ladies were the least bit magical before joining with their vampire mates. "She always had a way with plants, but she didn't really find out why until she started hanging out in the forest. Or so she said."

"That must've been interesting," Morgan replied, hoping to hear more, but willing to let the ladies take the conversation in whatever direction they wished.

Sadly, the conversation turned to other things, and somehow, they started talking about Christy and how she knew Matt best out of all of them. There were some not-so-subtle looks being thrown around between the friends, indicating clearly to Morgan that Matt had more...intimate knowledge of Sebastian's mate than she might have suspected.

"Sally has the most magic of our small group of friends, but Christy has some mad skills," Lissa confided. "She can already shapeshift, and she has the agility of a cat, not to mention the martial arts skills. *Sensei* Hiro has been training all of us, but Christy is really the best at everything. Kelly and I try not to be too jealous."

"It was necessary," Kelly said in a sober sort of voice. "You know that. Christy needed it, and Sebastian put her needs before his own in the most selfless act imaginable." Kelly's voice was soft and filled with understanding as she reached a hand out to her friend.

Christy took Kelly's hand and a sad smile passed between them. Morgan wondered what they were referencing, but even though she knew a lot about the Brotherhood and the new mates of her employers and friends, there were many aspects of their lives that they kept—understandably—to themselves.

Morgan had been involved in Christy's divorce from a hateful, violent man, but beyond knowledge of Christy's first marriage and its dissolution, Morgan didn't know all that much. She had just assumed Sebastian had discovered Christy was his One after turning her to save her life, but she didn't know the particulars. What the women were implying seemed a bit of a stretch. She hated to ask, but she was a cat and she was naturally curious...

"What did he do?" Morgan whispered, asking despite her best intentions not to pry.

It was Lissa who answered. "Sebastian arranged for Christy's first meal to be shifter blood. Matt's, to be precise. He held off consummating their relationship until he was certain Christy would be strong enough to face her past and never be frightened of a man again." Morgan must have frowned because Lissa went on. "A vampire's first meal is the most important of his or her existence. Kelly and I were converted more or less in the usual way, where our mate's blood was the first we ever tasted. Our mates are ancient and powerful, so we get a measure of their strength. And being mates, we also have a psychic connection that helps us learn things directly from their minds, at times. It's pretty awesome." Lissa smiled and sent a wink across the room to her husband, who smiled back at her.

"But Christy had been through a lot. Sebastian arranged for her to have Matt's magical blood a few times before he tested their attraction to find out if she truly was his One," Kelly picked up the story. "Shifter blood is like supercharged or something, according to Marc. It gives us some of the traits of the shifter and some of their strength, for a time. It's potent stuff. And having it for her first meal, Christy got some of Matt's cougar agility and stamina on a much longer term basis—possibly permanently. When she shifts, she can become a cat."

"A housecat," Christy quipped with good natured humor. "That was the first form I chose. The guys laughed at me." The other ladies chuckled with her.

For Morgan's part, she was too appalled at the ideas that were running through her head to speak. She knew enough about vampires to know that they usually fucked when they fed. So, if Matt had allowed Christy to bite him, he had probably been inside her, at the time. From all accounts—multiple times.

The mangy alley cat.

"Lissa and I might take decades, or even centuries, to build up the kind of power and control necessary to shapeshift," Kelly went on, apparently oblivious to Morgan's inner turmoil. "But, by biting a shifter, Christy got that skill early. She also moves like a cat and can leap to heights that are kind of awesome."

Christy blushed, even as she smiled and ducked her head.

Morgan had always liked Christy. Knowing what she did about her past and having dealt with her asshole of an ex-husband during the divorce, Morgan had developed a soft spot for the woman. She had felt like they had things in common.

But learning that, in all likelihood, Christy had slept with Matt—more than once—all feelings of comradeship were fading. Jealousy was springing up, making Morgan's inner cat want to yowl and claw. *Down, kitty.*

Appalled by both her reaction and the implications of Matt's hound dog ways, she avoided his eye for the rest of the night. It was just safer that way.

But she couldn't avoid him on the walk back to their cars, an hour later. After the plans had been picked apart and approved by the Brotherhood and the conversation had turned casual, Matt and Morgan finally took their leave. The vampires might be awake all night, but even shifters needed a little sleep before facing the new day.

And so, they found themselves walking back up to the office in the dark. The night closing around them in a way that made Morgan want to sprint away from the confusing man at her side. Her attraction to him hadn't faded, even after learning what she had tonight. Matt slept around, and while that shouldn't bother her because most shifters were a tad promiscuous before finding their mates, the fact that he'd slept with Christy—someone Morgan knew and liked—just struck a raw nerve.

Why it should matter so much to her, Morgan didn't really want to examine.

"Where's the fire?" Matt asked from slightly behind her.

She turned on him. "What?"

"You're practically jogging. I just wondered where the fire was that you had to get to so fast." He smiled in that disarming, totally charming way he had, but she was doing her best to resist. "It's a beautiful night. We've both had a long day. Slow down and relax a little. Why the rush?"

Angry that she'd let her inner turmoil show, even the tiniest bit, she slowed her fast pace and allowed him to catch up. She was a lawyer. She didn't show emotion when facing an adversary. And, sadly, Matt Redstone had, somehow, become her adversary, even though ultimately, they were working on the same side.

"Guess I was just thinking too hard." She tried to sound casual, but even to her own ears, she sounded more brittle than bored.

Matt reached into his pocket and pulled out some change. Picking out a shiny, copper coin, he handed it to her.

"What's this for?"

"It's a penny. You know...for your thoughts?" There was that charming smile again.

She felt like she was under Borg attack. *Resistance is futile.*

But she *had* to resist.

She handed the penny back to him. "I'm not sure they're even worth that much. You'd better keep your money." *And your charm and everything else.*

But he didn't cooperate. He took her hand and folded the penny into her fingers, wrapping his big hands around her fist.

"Keep it. For luck."

The air around them suddenly grew intimate, and she was powerless to move. The haven of her car was only a few dozen yards away. Her fast pace had moved them swiftly from the mansion to the office, and escape was imminent, but she couldn't make her feet move.

"There's another traditional thing we do for luck..." Matt whispered as his head lowered toward hers. Again, she was powerless to resist.

Matt's lips found hers, and she was a goner.

She melted into his arms as his grip moved from her hand to her shoulders, pulling her tight against his hard body. She felt...right. So many things felt like they clicked into place, but it couldn't be. Matt Redstone was a player. A dominant Alpha male who seemed to think any woman was his for the taking.

He did kiss like a dream, though. The arguments against him faded as his tongue moved in to take possession of her mouth. Her blood began to heat in explosive ways, her body thrumming with…something.

Matt pulled back and looked deep into her eyes.

"There, now. That's better," he whispered, as if he was gentling some wild animal.

The cat inside her—the traitor—sat up and allowed his voice to stroke her ruffled fur. She wanted to roll around in his scent and let his hands stroke her all over. The woman wanted more of his kiss.

Morgan initiated it, this time, going back for more of the exquisite torture that made her feel things she had never experienced before with any of her human boyfriends. She'd never been with a shifter. She'd never even been this close to a shifter before. Matt was a totally new experience for her, and she was very much afraid he was addictive.

She kissed him for all she was worth, practically climbing his body like a scratching post, surrounding him and being surrounded by his warmth, his scent, his incredible masculinity. This, her inner cat purred, this was an Alpha male worthy of the name.

Passion rose between them. She felt the excitement running through her veins as never before. She also felt the hardness of his cock against her belly. Even with layers of fabric between them, he was formidable. And then, she purred…

Holy shit!

She tore herself out of his arms, breaking the kiss and stumbling back, away from him as he let her go.

To purr in human form was something incredibly significant to cat shifters. Even Morgan knew that. And, for just a split second there, she'd thought she'd felt an answering rumble coming from his chest.

Dear, sweet Goddess! It couldn't be happening.

Turning tail and running as if the hounds of hell were on her heels probably wasn't the bravest thing she'd ever done, but Morgan did it. She ran all the way back to her car, glad as she had never been before that she didn't have to mess with keys. Her keyless entry and ignition were a blessing of technology that allowed her to get in the car and go, go, go!

She had to get away from the threat of Matt Redstone and his devastating kisses. Her primitive responses had never been so potent. For shit sure, she had never purred in human form before. And she wasn't going to admit she had done so now.

Giving in to Matt's allure would be the beginning of the end to all she held dear. She didn't want to become some playboy alley cat's little woman. She'd worked too hard to get to where she was. She wasn't going to throw it all away for some man who had already slept with one of her friends.

No, siree. Matt was off the agenda. Damaged goods. Christy's sloppy seconds.

Morgan had to keep coming up with reasons why she shouldn't go back and discover just what it was about the man that made her purr. As she drove away, she saw him walking slowly to his car. He paused, leaning against his vehicle, watching as she reversed and then sped away. She didn't acknowledge him, but she knew he knew that she saw him. Damn.

She had to get out of here. She had to think. She had to forget that incredible kiss. And the purring. Most of all, she had to forget the purring.

Matt watched Morgan speed away. He sent a silent prayer up to the Goddess she would drive safely. She'd been in a state when she'd run from him, and he couldn't really blame her. Matt was confused as hell, too. Confused, amazed, and still incredibly turned on by what, after all, had only been a simple kiss.

But it had been a life-altering kiss, just the same. Matt had finally answered the question that had been plaguing him since that first brief encounter, way back when. He'd been wondering for a long time whether or not he'd imagined his reaction to meeting Morgan, for the first time.

Now, he didn't have to wonder, anymore. His instincts hadn't been off. There was something truly special about

Morgan.

Her kiss had made him purr, which among big cat shifters could mean only one thing...

He'd just found his mate.

CHAPTER FOUR

Morgan thought she was pretty successful in hiding from Matt Redstone over the next few days. She'd ducked him at the winery offices, working out of her downtown legal office, instead.

She had stayed informed about the progress of the new plans via Irma and her connections in the local planning office. She knew the new plans had been accepted, and Matt was busy coordinating the arrival of his work crews. They would be breaking ground today, in fact, and Atticus had specifically asked her to be on hand for the occasion.

Short of outright refusing a special request from her largest and very indulgent client, she would have to show up and make nice with all the *weres* at the construction site. And see Matt again...

She wasn't sure she could handle it. Her nerves were tied up in knots just thinking about it.

Yeah, the closer she drove to the construction site where the ceremony would be held, the more certain she became that she was making a big mistake. Her life had been just fine without *weres* in it up 'til now. She didn't need to make nice with the shifters, no matter what the Brotherhood thought. And she most especially didn't need to be anywhere near a particular *were*cougar anytime in the near future. Maybe not ever.

She almost turned her car around half a dozen times, but, then, she thought about Atticus's reaction. And his mate's. Lissa would tell her friends, and then, Christy might realize just why Morgan was behaving like such a scaredy cat. The green-eyed monster of jealousy had been riding her hard since that little get together at Atticus's home.

No way would Morgan give anyone the satisfaction of knowing how deeply the thoughts of Matt with other women—one incredibly beautiful vampire woman, in particular—hurt. She would not have them whispering behind her back. She would tough this out and put on a brave face. Nobody would have the satisfaction of seeing her crumble. Never again.

Bravado was just about the only thing holding her up as Morgan parked her car on the dirt in the area that had been cleared for construction equipment. It lay all over the small area, big yellow machines dormant for the moment, civilian cars mixed in with the trucks and life-size Tonka toys.

She didn't see any other people, yet, but when she opened her car door, the scents hit her. Wild. Wolf. Werewolf. And Others. She scented magic, too. Pure and good, its scent drawing her onwards, toward the center of the cluster of giant yellow machines.

As she rounded the first bulldozer, she was brought up short by the presence of a huge man. He stood a few feet from her, and she realized he was some sort of guard, looking out for strangers approaching the ceremonial site. He took a rather obvious sniff in her direction and relaxed marginally. Her instincts, and nose, said he was a werewolf. A big-assed werewolf with muscles on top of his muscles. The man was huge!

"You must be the lawyer," he said in a gruff voice, stepping back, out of her way. "Go right on through. I think they were waiting for you to show before they got started."

The man mountain even smiled at her, a slight baring of teeth that made her edge past him quickly. If this guy was any indication of what lay beyond the inner circle of equipment, Morgan had been right to be afraid. These *weres* were built on the massive side, and their every movement spoke of strength and the ability to tear her apart with a single swipe of one enormous paw.

Morgan did her best not to show her fear, but he probably scented a bit of her adrenaline. Hopefully, he'd put it up to the start he'd given her when he suddenly appeared. She didn't want this big predator to know she was afraid. Surprised was okay. But fearful just wouldn't cut it.

"Thanks," she said briskly, wrapping her mantle of false bravado back around herself. She walked away from the smiling werewolf and around another giant machine and then...

She was in the center of a ceremonial circle. Not just a circle formed by big yellow machines, but something that had been set up with torches at every cardinal point and an altar at the center.

And at the altar, stood the priestess Marc had tried to get Morgan to talk to many times in the past. Hilda. The priestess who served the entire Northern California region since her predecessor's death. It was too much territory for one woman—or so Marc had insisted many times.

That little fact had worked in Morgan's favor. Hilda hadn't had enough time in Napa to track Morgan down and make her talk. And no way was Morgan going to seek out the woman with the spooky gray eyes to bear her soul. Some things were just too damn painful to rehash over and over. It was bad enough that Marc knew most of what had happened to Morgan. And Morgan was fine now. No reason to go raking up old trauma for shits and giggles.

Hilda saw her as the rest of the gathered *weres* turned to look at Morgan. They were standing in concentric circles. The outermost circle was made up of burly male werewolves, like the guy who'd been guarding the perimeter. The inner circle held Jenny's family, plus a few younger male wolves who looked like teenagers, probably just starting to work with the older men on the construction crews.

At the center, directly around the altar, stood Hilda, Jenny and Matt.

And everyone—*everyone*—was now looking at Morgan. Talk about making an entrance. Morgan cringed inwardly.

"Good, you're here. Now, we can begin," Hilda said in a cheery voice, as if every set of eyes in the entire gathering weren't sizing up the newcomer. "Come over here, Morgan. You're taking one of the cardinal points to represent the Brotherhood."

It was mid-afternoon, so it was obvious that none of the vampires could attend this particular ceremony, though she was pretty sure they'd come at dusk to do whatever Hilda might ask of them. Morgan hadn't quite thought far enough ahead to realize that the priestess would be involved in this. Morgan had foolishly believed this was going to be like a human groundbreaking ceremony, with speeches and shovels of dirt flying for photo ops.

What it really was, was some kind of mystical, magical mumbo jumbo with fire and altars and cardinal points…and a priestess. Morgan should have seen it coming, but maybe it was a touch of willful blindness on her part that hadn't let her think things through. These homes were being built for shifters. Of course there was going to be more to the story than simply digging a little dirt for the cameras.

Resigned to her fate, Morgan made her way through the silent rings of shifters, heading for the altar.

"Good to see you again, Morgan," Hilda said quietly as she approached. "I've given you the South for Fire." Hilda nodded to a spot, opposite Matt. Morgan hadn't looked straight at him, yet, and avoided it, now, but they would be standing opposite each other, the altar between them. "Matt is Earth. I'm Air, and Jenny is Water," Hilda continued. "I chose these designations for each of us because of your unique natures. Jenny is the mother energy. She has learned to flow and adapt like water, and her strength builds slowly but is nearly unstoppable."

Morgan privately thought Hilda was giving Jenny a bit of a pep talk with those words. Morgan looked at the female werewolf and saw her take heart from the priestess's comments. Hilda was, no doubt, good at her job, but Morgan had never given the woman a chance to try on her. Morgan silently hoped Hilda wasn't going to turn that analytical gaze on her next.

Morgan breathed a little sigh of relief when Hilda picked on Matt instead.

"Matt is Earth, because like the earth, he is strong and supportive. He is deeply rooted and stable. He has seen and done much and has remained firm and unyielding." Morgan resolved not to look at Matt, instead focusing on Hilda. She was caught by those eerie gray eyes when Hilda turned to her. "And you, Morgan, have been through fire. You know its pains and its triumphs. Your spirit lights our way."

Hilda released her, turning away, and Morgan fought not to droop. Thank the Goddess that was over. She counted herself lucky to have escaped a more thorough explanation of the *fire* she'd been through. Morgan didn't know how much Marc had told Hilda, but it was clear her guardian had blabbed at least a little bit to the priestess. Darn it.

Hilda told them all to hold hands, and Morgan was glad she wasn't directly next to Matt. She didn't have to hold his hand—just the priestess's and Jenny's. What followed was a lot of chanting and words that Morgan mostly tuned out. She had never been big on ceremonies and had never been involved with the shifter side of religion all that much. Her mother had taught her to respect the Goddess, but that was about it. In fact, Morgan had never met a priestess before Marc had introduced her to Hilda.

Morgan woke up a bit when she felt the buildup of power. Her senses crackled as Hilda's words seemed to draw strength from the slowly moving circles of shifters. The elements seemed to answer Hilda's call as Morgan swore for a moment she could feel the fire of the torches burning through her and into the hands she held, circulating and returning, then collecting in Hilda to be redirected into whatever magic she was working.

Morgan felt the earth shake slightly under her feet as the altar stone began to move downward. Her gaze shot upward, meeting Matt's without her conscious permission. His topaz eyes held her mesmerized as wind whipped up around them. And then, rain splashed them as a tiny tempest concentrated its power just within the circle and focused on the altar stone. Water coalesced on it and rolled down its sides as it moved downward into the straining earth.

Suddenly, it pushed into the ground at their feet with a final, reverberating bang, and then, the tiny storm lifted, and the daylight shone down on them, once again. Morgan was left stunned, saying nothing as Hilda finished up her chant and dismissed the power she had collected, putting it into the stone.

Morgan took a good look at the stone and realized it wasn't really an altar, at all. It was a cornerstone. A highly magical one now.

Once again, Morgan had had no idea that shifters did such things. They'd just laid the cornerstone for one of the main buildings in the project. Something Matt called a Pack house. Being unfamiliar with werewolf society, Morgan wasn't quite sure what such a thing might be used for, but if they were starting the new community with this structure—and putting that much magic into it—it had to be pretty important.

The circles of shifters broke up, and someone moved the torches over to a small group of tables where refreshments had been set up. The ceremony quickly turned into a little party, with Jenny's family mixing with the construction crews as if they were old friends. And they probably were, Morgan realized. They had moved from Las Vegas to Napa only in the past year, leaving behind their wolf Pack and wolfie friends for this unknown situation.

"You all did really well." Hilda's bright voice came to Morgan as she watched the werewolves. She was still standing in her place by the stone, as were the others. She felt a little sluggish, but she guessed that probably had to do with the magic that had just been flowing through her. "You might feel a little residual tingle, for a few hours," Hilda cautioned, "but you all played your parts like pros. The cornerstone is set, and set well. This is a really great start for the new community." Hilda turned to Jenny and walked with her toward the refreshments.

Morgan was glad to see the priestess go. Hilda made her uncomfortable.

And speaking of uncomfortable... Matt moved to stand directly in front of her, his arms folded, his gaze almost...hurt? No way. She had to be imagining that.

"You've been avoiding me," he accused. There. That was more like it.

"I've been busy," she replied, reminding herself to stand tall. She wasn't going to let anyone—especially him—see her as weak.

Matt just eyed her for a moment, then sighed and backed off a bit. "Okay. Whatever. Look, we need to work together. There are things we still have to do to make this project happen."

"I'm at your disposal for this project," she repeated the party line. Atticus had said as much, and she would do the work he paid her to do—but no more.

"Fine," he ground out, then switched modes to strictly business. Good. She could handle that. Couldn't she? "I think you need to organize a meeting with the ecological protest group. We need to show them what we have planned and get them on board, if at all possible. We don't want any more bad press."

He had a point. And, if she'd been thinking clearly at all the past few days, she would have already done it. Damn. She'd been walking around in a daze since that night. She really had to get a grip.

"All right. I'll work on it tomorrow and call you with the details once I have something. Can we give them a tour of the new property?"

She began walking, and he followed her, even though she wasn't heading for the refreshments. No, the sooner she got out of here, the better. She couldn't handle all these *weres*. She was a loner and wanted to keep it that way.

"Yeah, that sounds like a good idea. We can have some of the trails laid out by tomorrow, so they can see what we've got in mind." He seemed to be thinking as he walked. "And I'll do up some renderings that'll showcase the wild space. We can probably give them a nice little packet with environmental impact numbers and all kinds of design specs for the public spaces. That ought to impress them."

"Sounds good." They were at the perimeter of machines, and Matt's steps began to slow.

There was no way she was going to stay here one minute longer. He'd just have to deal with her by phone.

"I'll call you as soon as I have something. Bye." She turned and fled.

She had a feeling he was watching her every move, but she couldn't stop herself. She had to get out of there now. Or ten minutes ago. Yeah, ten minutes ago would have been better, but she'd settle for now.

She scrambled to her car and started that sucker up as soon as her ass hit the leather seat. Within moments, she was headed down the road as fast as she dared. She'd had about all she could take of *were* togetherness for one day.

* * *

Matt spoke with Morgan only once, briefly, two days later. She'd managed to set up a meeting with the eco group for the next day, and he cleared his afternoon to spend with the self-proclaimed eco warriors.

He wished he could've gotten more time with Morgan, but she was shutting him out completely. He figured it was his past coming back to haunt him, but he'd given it a lot of thought, and he really couldn't see how he could've done anything differently. If she was going to be upset with him for having been with Christy—which is what he believed to be the cause of her avoidance—there was nothing he could do to change the past. He'd had his reasons for answering Sebastian's request to let Christy feed from him, and they went a lot deeper than just momentary hedonism.

If only he could explain to Morgan. If only she'd give him a chance to tell her why he'd chosen to do what he'd done.

But she wouldn't even give him the time of day, right now. He figured he'd give her a bit of time to cool off before he pushed his luck any further. He'd be in Napa for some time yet, working on this project. Grif had asked him to stay until things were well underway, and Matt planned to be even more conscientious than usual on this particular job. Anything that would keep him close to Morgan.

Hell, he could always come right out and tell Grif why he wanted to stay in California a while longer. He knew his brother would give him free reign—especially if Matt hinted at a possible mating—but he really didn't want to deal with the teasing or the grief he would get from his four older brothers if they realized why he was so keen on Napa all of a sudden. Not to mention the humiliation if he didn't manage to talk Morgan around and had to go home empty handed.

Matt went out to the site of the proposed nature reserve early, policing the site for trash and scouting the perimeter. He wanted everything to be perfect for the eco guys. The small but vocal group could cause a lot of trouble for them if they decided to launch a media campaign against the project.

Everything could still get put on indefinite hold if the human community turned too much attention on the project. Matt didn't want that to happen, for any number of reasons, not least of which was because he didn't want to disappoint Jenny. The poor woman had been through a lot in recent years. She was finally finding some happiness again, and Matt wanted to make sure she was as comfortable as he could possibly make her.

The housing project would do that. Which was why he had to make it happen. Forget all the money and time invested in this project already. What really mattered most in life was people. And Jenny and her tiny Pack of females were good people. They deserved a fresh start in a comfortable, safe place. Matt would move heaven and earth to give it to them.

By the appointed time for the meeting, Matt had gone over every inch of the acreage set aside for the preserve. He'd met the local wildlife, which included some skittish deer, a few raccoons, possums, a skunk family, and assorted squirrels. There was also a wide range of birds, from a predator hawk pair, what he thought was probably an owl's nest, and many, many smaller birds from woodpeckers to chickadees. He'd found the natural stream that ran through the property and the small pond that was home to a few ducks.

He thought he had a pretty good handle on the wildlife and the lay of the land. He'd take the eco nuts on a tour and point out all the natural beauty of the spot and give them precise details about the small changes they would make to mark off trails for the humans who wanted to partake of the natural beauty of the spot. He had it all planned out, with little presentation folders Irma had helped him prepare for each guest.

What he hadn't prepared for all that well was the surly attitude of the group as they arrived en masse in an old, beat up van that smelled of French fries and Mexican food. The thing reeked of the grease they used to fuel it, and Matt had to find a place to stand upwind of the monstrosity.

Morgan parked right behind the eco van and greeted Matt frostily as he did his best not to gag on the smell of the eco guys' bio-fuel. He handed out the prepared materials and tried to learn everyone's names, but the odor of the fuel was clogging his sensitive nose and making him want to sneeze. Badly. He had to get them on the trail, and that's what he did, right away, deciding to do his presentation as they walked, rather than talk and then walk.

Slight change of plans, but he was good about rolling with

the punches. He led the group out, ignoring, for the moment, their antagonistic attitude. With time, and some well-placed information, he hoped to change their attitudes. He put his best foot forward and began to speak about the land and their plans for it while Morgan brought up the rear of the small group, saying nothing.

When they arrived at the pond, Matt invited everyone to sit on a log he had pre-positioned and staged to look as if it had been there for years. The eco guys seemed to buy it, a couple of the females remarking on the ducks and one adventurous soul examining the various mushrooms that liked to grow in the area.

Matt decided to stop here. What better spot? It was free of the French fry smell of their biodiesel, and the flora and fauna were already doing their best to enchant the newcomers into a better mood.

He began talking about the project and did his best to paint a picture with his words. He noted Morgan's every move, but he did his best to concentrate on the human audience, impressing upon them how much he loved the land and how little he wanted to change what nature had done here so beautifully.

"We're going to put in marked trails of varying skill levels and a waste bin at the trailhead, which will be checked daily, but other than that..." he said as he was wrapping up his discussion of the nature preserve, "...we'll leave Mother Nature to do what she does best."

"What about security?" the leader of the group asked. His name was Daryl, and he was the owner of the French fry mobile. "Since this is private land, have you given any thought to private park rangers or some kind of ready assistance if a hiker gets in trouble?"

"Actually, we have. Several of the families that will be moving into the housing development are naturalists. There's one man, in particular, who is a retired Yellowstone Park Ranger."

Matt knew exactly which of the wolves would be moving

to Napa to form the nucleus of a small Pack along with Jenny and her family. Mostly, the spots were going to retirees and women like Jenny who wanted to work, just not in construction.

"His name is William O'Donnel, and you have his bio in the materials I've provided. He's already agreed to set up a private patrol based on his years with the National Parks Service. He'll be working directly for the Maxwell Preserve Trust that has been set up to fund this preserve, with the stated goal of adding to these lands, if possible, over the next several decades. As adjacent lands come up for sale, the Trust aims to bid on them, trying to expand the natural area as much as we can."

Matt saw nods from the eco warriors, and he knew they hadn't expected that particular feature. Score one for Morgan. It had been her idea to set up the Preserve Trust and give it a mission of buying up the land in the area. Atticus had approved the idea, loving the thought of creating an even larger buffer between his lands and his neighbors.

Atticus's vineyard was on the edge of the valley. The housing development was a short distance away, in the rocky areas that were no good for growing grapes. If they had their way, the nature preserve was going to work its way up the hills behind the vineyard as much as possible over the next decades. Before too much longer, the vampire vintner would own as much land as he could possibly buy up—all very legitimately—turning it into a nature preserve and ensuring his privacy.

Morgan had worked it all out so that he actually gained tax breaks by donating the money to the trust as a charitable contribution. She was clever, was Morgan.

"This is all great, and we like the idea of the preserve, but our main problem has been, and continues to be, the old gold mine." Daryl got to the crux of the group's objections. "We're concerned that, if you stir up the land nearby, all the old tailings will cause problems downstream."

Matt was ready for this question. "If you'll look at the

revised plans filed and approved a few days ago with the county, you'll see that the gold mine is going to be sealed off. Absolutely nothing of the old mine will be used in the new construction. The most we're going to do is stabilize the area by sealing the mine entrance permanently. In fact, our guys have already started. We can hike up there next and take a look at their progress, if you want." The eco group seemed surprised by the news, and most of them looked pleased.

The spokesman looked skeptical. "I'd say we should definitely go up there. I want to see for myself what kind of methods you're employing."

Matt expected that and had his crews working on the main entrance to the mine, which would be closed permanently. The secret plans had nothing to do with the very obvious main entrance, and never had. There were other shafts. Other entrances that could be created much closer to the housing development, in much greater secrecy.

He also wanted to give the eco guys one more aspect to think about. "There will be children living in the new housing. Babies and youngsters. We don't want any of them wandering into an unsafe situation. Nor do we want to stir up any toxins that might be in the area. We plan to do even more environmental testing than the results already in your handouts. And, if any new problems are discovered, a full cleanup will be done in accordance with California and EPA law, so that the land is returned to its natural, safe state. Testing will occur on an ongoing basis, and any new situations will be remediated before any construction will proceed or anyone will be allowed to move in. Redstone takes this stuff very seriously. I know you may not be familiar with our company, since we haven't done too many public projects around here recently, but we have the highest rankings in safety and environmental responsibility. We pride ourselves on that, and on our respect for Mother Earth."

Well, that was no fib. The Redstones followed the Goddess. Some people called her Mother Earth, but Matt believed it didn't matter what you called Her, as long as you did right by Her.

"Shall we hike up to the old mine entrance, now?" Matt stood and the others followed suit.

Again, he led the small party up through the woods, pointing out markers he'd laid out earlier for what would be one of the lightly groomed hiking trails. Before too much longer, they arrived at the site where one of his work crews had already set up. Matt gave the group a quick safety briefing for being on an active construction site then kitted them out with plastic orange vests and hard hats before allowing them closer to inspect the methods and work progress that had already been made.

This particular crew was run by an Alpha female werewolf named Philomena. Matt asked her to say a few words and describe the methods the crew had been employing. She seemed to impress the male members of the human group, just as Matt had hoped. Philomena's natural leadership and command presence was tempered by her sultry looks and soft-spoken demeanor. Her dominance was clear. She didn't have to shout to get her point across. Matt had always liked that about her, and it seemed the humans were even more enchanted with the tall brunette.

Matt stayed back and let Philomena do her thing, hoping he'd finally get a chance to talk with Morgan. She'd done her best to steer clear of him so far, hanging in the rear of the group and avoiding eye contact, but he wasn't going to pass up this opportunity when she could so easily evade him again, once this dog and pony show was over.

CHAPTER FIVE

Morgan had to admit, Matt was a good speaker. He had the situation well in hand, and though the meeting had started out with more than a bit of animosity on the part of the eco group, Matt now had them eating out of his hands. Having the female wolf lead the tour of the construction site had been a stroke of genius. Most of the human males were watching the sexy wolf woman with something close to worship in their eyes, and even the human females in the group responded to her natural authority. The human women wanted to be her, while the human men, no doubt, wanted to *do* her.

Morgan had to stifle a little snicker as she made the joke in her head. She also had to revise some of her thoughts about werewolves and how women were treated in the Pack structure. Before seeing Philomena in action, Morgan had had no idea there were female wolves working in such powerful roles.

Maybe it was something unique to wolves? Or maybe Matt hadn't been exaggerating when he described the way things worked in the Redstone Clan. She wasn't sure, but she was definitely intrigued by this female Alpha wolf. Morgan would try to find time to speak with Philomena, if at all possible. Such a strong female would tell Morgan the truth about how things really were in the shifter world, she was certain.

"At last, we're alone," Matt's voice came from behind. The bastard had snuck up on her when she was busy thinking and observing Philomena in action. Dammit.

She began walking, striking out after the tour group. "Don't think so."

"Morgan…" He followed after her, hustling to keep up with her brisk strides. "Look, I know you're upset with me, but can't we at least talk about it?"

She rounded on him. "There's nothing to talk about." She was going to do her best to brazen it out. She did *not* want to get into an emotional conversation out here in the middle of a work site with dozens of sharp werewolf ears listening in.

"I think there is," he argued. "Morgan, we need to work together, and it's damn hard to do that if you won't talk to me."

"I'm talking to you. I set up this damn meeting. I've been working with you. Don't you pull that crap on me. What I don't have to do is be your best friend. They don't pay me enough for that." She sounded like a shrew, but she couldn't help herself. Jealousy had been eating her alive for the past few days, and it made her temper flare into places best left alone.

A wolf snickered nearby, and she realized the damn construction crew really was listening in on them. Well, so be it. At least they weren't snickering at her. That one had been aimed directly at Matt because of what she'd said about him.

In one way, she felt bad about treating him like this in public, but in another, he was getting only what he deserved. The horny bastard.

But he turned the tables on her. He stepped closer and snaked one arm around her waist, pulling her against his body. Her breath left in a whoosh as surprise turned to something a lot hotter…and a lot less controllable. Damn the man.

"I don't want to just be your friend, Morgan. I want something much more important from you." His lips came closer, and she was powerless in his hold. It was as if her brain went on a little vacation while her body just gave in to what it really wanted. This man. Holding her. Doing things to her...

Dammit!

"Sorry to interrupt," came a tentative voice from off to one side.

Matt let her go and turned on a dime to face the newcomer. Had a human really just snuck up on two *were*cats without either one of them noticing? Wow.

That only went to prove how dangerous this man was to her equilibrium. Matt was not a calming influence. Not like Marc and his Brotherhood cohorts.

Morgan turned to see one of the eco women standing about six feet away, shuffling from one foot to the other, clearly uncomfortable. A low growl came from deep in Matt's chest. Hopefully, it was too low for human hearing. Morgan tapped Matt on the shoulder, edging him aside so she could meet the human girl's eyes.

"No problem," Morgan said brightly, pushing through her embarrassment at being caught in a compromising situation. Truthfully, she was thankful to the human woman for putting a stop to something that could have easily gone a little too far. Morgan had been *that* close to succumbing to Matt's nearness. In truth, she'd been ready to pounce on the man and kiss him, if he didn't do it first. "What can I do for you?" she asked her unlikely human savior.

The woman stepped closer as Morgan approached. She noted Matt, close behind and to one side, ready to defend Morgan if the human proved dangerous in some way. Overprotective shifter males were something Morgan expected, but Matt was at least allowing her to meet the girl halfway, even if he was still on guard. She'd give him a point for that, at least.

"I didn't want to say this in front of the others, but there are some really bad vibes coming out of the mine," the woman said in a rush. "I know you probably think I'm crazy, but I'm kind of sensitive to bad juju, and this place has it in spades." The human paused, cringing a little as she looked into Morgan's eyes, probably hoping Morgan wouldn't laugh at her.

"I'm listening," Morgan said with calm authority to which the human responded. Relief crossed the woman's almost elfin-looking face. The woman had red hair and freckles. She was probably of Irish descent, if Morgan was any judge. "What's your name?"

"I'm Rosalie," the human answered, stepping forward to offer her hand for a quick shake. Morgan took it and felt a little jolt of…something…from the woman. Rosalie's blue eyes widened, and then, a smile spread over her face.

"Oh. I get it now. You're one of the forest spirits. You *will* take care of this land," she whispered, then nodded slightly to herself. She shook her head as she let go of Morgan's hand, and then, she frowned. "You need to know that there are people up here—underground. Bad people. Doing bad things. The mine is being defiled, and the earth is crying out for help. I can hear it rumble. And, if these people aren't stopped, the earth will rise."

Morgan was instantly alert. The woman didn't sound crazy. In fact, she sounded all too sane. And gifted. Some humans were. There were magic users in many races of humans, but the Irish seemed to be particularly endowed. It was almost certain this Rosalie had some ability with magic.

Matt stepped closer. "Earthquakes?" he asked in a deep, concerned voice.

Rosalie nodded at him. "And worse." She looked from Morgan to Matt and back again. "You're one, too, aren't you?" She didn't wait for an answer before looking quickly at the small portion of the construction crew that had formed a rough, protective semi-circle around the trio. The wolves were always on guard, it seemed. "And so are your people." Rosalie smiled gently. "Okay. I see this place is in good hands. I'll talk to the rest of the group and get them to leave you guys alone. Believe it or not, they listen to me." She chuckled a bit. "You won't get any more trouble about the housing. I know your kind holds the earth and Her creatures sacred, like we do."

"What will you tell them?" Morgan wanted to know.

"Oh, don't worry. They don't know about you, and they won't hear it from me. There are many things the rest of humanity isn't ready to know."

"How do *you* know?" Matt asked, his eyes narrowed on the woman.

"My gram was from the old country, and I inherited a bit of her gift. She taught me. I know we're special, and that you are, too, though I don't know much more than that. My family isn't as powerful as they once were, generations ago. Too much marrying for love." A smile graced her lips. "But we wouldn't have it any other way. Love is more important than bloodlines and power, right?"

"I couldn't agree more," Matt said, surprising Morgan. "Rosalie, if you don't mind, I'd love to put you in touch with a woman I know named Hilda Birgo. She might be able to help you learn a bit more about the things you don't yet know, if you want that."

Rosalie seemed to consider, tilting her head in a quizzical fashion for a moment. Then, she smiled. "I think I'd like that." She pulled out her mobile phone. "I'll beam you my deets."

Matt reached into his pocket, and they exchanged information quickly. Then, Rosalie sobered.

"You will take what I said to heart, won't you?" She seemed truly worried. "I really believe there's some weird stuff going down in the mine. I can't do anything about it. I don't have anything like your power. But somebody needs to do something—especially if you're going to be building homes near here. If left unchecked, something bad is going to happen. I can feel it in my bones."

"We'll investigate," Matt assured the woman. "I promise."

Rosalie seemed relieved, but still worried. "Just be careful, okay?"

"Will do." Matt gave her one of his patented smiles, and the human woman seemed to calm. She smiled again and left them, walking back to her group.

Morgan noticed one of the werewolf men following Rosalie at a discreet distance and looking for all the world as if he wasn't deliberately tailing the woman. If Morgan hadn't seen Matt exchange quick, almost imperceptible nods with the wolf in question, she probably wouldn't have realized his casual walk took the wolf on a parallel course with Rosalie.

Morgan had no doubt the wolf would listen in on every word Rosalie spoke for the remainder of her visit. With his sharp shifter hearing, he wouldn't even have to be all that close to her to spy on her. Morgan knew it was necessary to keep an eye on the human, but she couldn't help feeling sympathetic to Rosalie, as well. In just the short time they'd spoken, Morgan had discovered she liked the red-headed human. She hoped Rosalie was on the level. Morgan thought she was, but the wolf following her around would make sure.

With a start, Morgan also realized that the wolf who was following Rosalie was the same mountain of a man who had blocked her path at the cornerstone laying ceremony. He was some sort of guard, Morgan thought. And perhaps an Alpha in his own right. He certainly was large enough. Morgan hoped the guy didn't inadvertently scare the bejeezus out of the petite woman. If she caught on to the fact that she was being observed, that giant wolf just might freak her out.

"Are you sure that's wise?" Morgan asked, watching the two walk away, seemingly independent of each other.

"She has to be watched," Matt said quietly. "You know that."

"Yeah, I get that, but that big wolf is likely to scare the crap out of her if she realizes. And she's pretty sharp for a human." Morgan still kept her eye on the woman, who had just rejoined the tour group.

"Magic user," Matt corrected her. "Even if she only has a bit of the gift, she's still a mage. And don't worry about Neil. He looks scary—and he is scary—but I'd trust him with my baby sister. He wouldn't hurt a woman. Not by a long shot. He comes from a family dominated by females. You see…Philomena is his mom."

Morgan blinked. "Are you kidding me?" She could hardly reconcile the sexy Alpha female who ran the crew as being the mountainous man's mother.

"Come on." He turned toward her, a teasing smile on his face. "You know we don't age like humans. You've been living in their world too long if you can't wrap your head around a sexy, century-old mom of six being Alpha of her little Pack and running a construction crew."

"Six?" Morgan gulped. Maybe she had been hanging out with humans too long.

"Neil is the youngest. I think that's why we became friends. I've got four older brothers. He's got five older sisters. It's not easy being the youngest in a crowd." Matt looked to where the big werewolf was working on a piece of equipment well within shifter hearing range of the human group. "Four of his sisters are mated with cubs of their own. The fifth is Cindy. Have you met her, yet?" Matt didn't wait for an answer. "She's the Beta of this crew. She's got every bit of the Alpha potential of her mother—as does Neil—but like me, they want to keep working with their family, so they play subordinate roles to their mom. In my case, I answer to Grif, as do the rest of my brothers. He's the oldest, so he's the Alpha in charge of it all, though he uses each of us to oversee different parts of the Clan and the business—which, sometimes, works out to be one and the same."

"What about their father?" Morgan asked, curious about the family.

Matt sighed and the sound held real regret. "He's gone. Killed in a freak accident about ten years ago. This whole crew was working for a different construction firm, back then. Safety wasn't exactly a priority, and ol' Ben got crushed by a piece of falling iron. There wasn't much anyone could do. He died pretty much instantly, Goddess bless him."

Morgan sent up the same blessing silently, feeling for the

family.

"They were all working with the crew, then, including the four older sisters. They were gathered around him when he passed, which I think was a good thing, in a way, even if it was traumatic for them. He went out surrounded by those he loved most." Matt went silent, for a moment, then continued, "Their whole crew is made up of extended family—cousins, in-laws and such. They're very close knit, even for wolves, and Ben was their Alpha. Philomena was his second, and she stepped up to run the crew after he passed. She decided to break with the other company and seek out Redstone. Grif met with her, first, then we all got to meet the rest of the crew and realized they'd be a good fit for our company, and our Clan. They moved over to Redstone and have been with us ever since. Two of Philomena's daughters and their families want to move into this housing development and seek work at the winery, so they all have a vested interest, beyond the usual, in making sure this development is top notch."

The conversation lagged a bit as Morgan contemplated all she had learned. She might've been very wrong about how shifters really lived. These wolves certainly had no problem taking orders from a woman, and Philomena had really impressed Morgan with how capable and intelligent she was, and the way everyone looked up to her and followed her orders. Philomena was no *little woman* to be kept barefoot and pregnant—even if she'd had six children already.

No, Philomena seemed more the type to strap her baby in a papoose and bring them along to wherever she was working at the time. Philomena was an Alpha female truly worthy of the name, and Morgan had to admit she might even have a tiny case of hero worship for the woman. Morgan kinda wanted to be like that when she "grew up". She had to chuckle at her own thoughts.

"So…" Matt turned back to her, his expression serious. Morgan stifled her amusement and got back to the business at hand. "What do we do about Rosalie's warning?"

"Like you said—we investigate," Morgan said without hesitation.

"Agreed. But when?" Matt looked around the active site. "And where?"

"There are other access points that aren't quite so obvious," Morgan offered.

"And tomorrow is Saturday. I've given the crews the weekend off since we're not really in full swing, yet, and they're all still settling in. The less people around, the easier it'll be to spot strangers. And, if someone is covertly accessing the mine, they're more likely to do so when the crews aren't here."

"Good point," Morgan agreed. "So tomorrow then?"

* * *

Morgan thought again about how she'd come to be lurking near one of the side shafts that led down into the mine on Saturday morning. She had resolved less than twenty-four hours ago to steer clear of Matt Redstone, but yet, there they were, on an honest-to-Goddess stakeout. He'd even brought along a box of donuts. Because, he'd said, it couldn't be a real stakeout without donuts.

After about five minutes of sitting, waiting for something to happen, she'd given in and opened the box. Of the dozen donuts that had been in the little pink and orange box, only about three were left. Thank goodness shifters had fast metabolisms.

The spot they'd chosen to watch from was a short distance up the side of the mountain, looking down on three sides of the property. There was enough vegetation to hide their presence, as long as they were stealthy. Morgan had worn a long-sleeved hunter green top and brown pants, but Matt had opted for camo.

"You look like a TV duck hunter," she observed. "All you're missing is the scraggily beard."

Matt patted his pockets in a searching manner then

stroked his smooth chin. "Sorry. I don't need a fancy call or shotgun to bag a duck. My claws do just fine. As for the beard. I have quite enough fur when I shift. I don't need even more when I'm on two legs. Besides...Mama taught us all to look after ourselves, which included living up to her idea of *clean cut*. You should've seen her when Grif and Steve came back from the desert with nomad beards. She made them go shave before she'd let them sit down at the dinner table." He chuckled at the memory.

"She sounds like a formidable woman," Morgan said softly.

"She was," he agreed. After a moment, he turned to look at her. "You know, I don't talk about her much. Her death was incredibly difficult for all of us in the family, but it feels good, now, to remember the good times we had with her. I wish you could've met her. She would've liked you a lot, Morgan."

Morgan wasn't sure what to say to that. He sounded so sincere, and the idea that he would've wanted her to meet his mother was kind of staggering. Could he possibly mean it that way? Like he *wanted her to meet his mother*? With all the connotations that carried in the human world?

She didn't know if such a thing was equivalent among shifters. She hadn't spent enough time among shifters to know all the little rules and etiquettes of their society. She decided to go for a polite, but noncommittal response.

"I think I would've liked her, too." As soon as the words were out of her mouth, Morgan realized the truth of them.

Everything she'd heard about the last Redstone Clan Matriarch had impressed Morgan. Both the few things Matt had told her about his mother and the information she'd been able to glean from the Brotherhood. Both Marc and Sebastian had been truly saddened to hear of Mrs. Redstone's death and had sent personal condolences to the family, as had the entire Brotherhood.

They had reminisced with Morgan about the woman, sharing memories of meeting with the Matriarch. She grilled them both about her son's unlikely friendship with a powerful group of bloodletters. Marc had said the Matriarch hadn't been the least bit afraid of him. She'd stood up to him, wanting to judge for herself what, and who, her son was getting mixed up with. Marc had said he wasn't even sure if Matt knew about his mother's meddling, but respected the Matriarch enough not to spill the beans.

Morgan privately thought maybe Marc was a little afraid of the woman, though he'd never admit such a thing out loud. He also seemed genuinely touched at the mother's love for her son. Morgan had known the Master long enough to be able to read between the lines of his words.

"Look..." Matt's soft voice drew her attention back to him. "I know there's an eight-hundred-pound gorilla sitting between us, and I'd like the chance to clear the air, once and for all. If you're still upset with me after that, then so be it, but I'd like to at least speak my piece."

Dammit. She really didn't want to venture into these shark-infested waters, but she'd had time to cool down, and she realized she probably wasn't being fair. She had to let him say what he wanted to say and just get it out of the way. She doubted anything he could tell her would change her mind about his character, but if hearing him out would get him to back off, then she could at least humor him.

"All right," she said with a sigh. "Say what you want to say. I won't stop you."

Matt looked at her, unease clear in his eyes. "I don't usually talk about this, either, but you need to know why I agreed to help Christy in that particular way. It wasn't what you're thinking." She snorted, and he shook his head. "Okay, maybe it was a little, but mostly..." He trailed off and looked away, scanning the land below.

She waited for him to speak, hoping he would just spit out what he wanted to say and be done with it. She wanted to end this conversation, but she knew she couldn't just walk away again. This had to come out before they could move on—she with her life and he with his.

"I had two sisters. Belinda is the youngest. She's just a teenager. But I also had an older sister named Jackie. I was still in school when she mated and moved to her mate's Clan. We didn't see her much after that, and we sure as hell didn't know what was going on in her marriage."

Matt ran a troubled hand through his golden hair, and Morgan frowned. What did this have to do with him having sex with Christy?

"Sometimes—very rarely—shifter matings are just…wrong. She hid it from everyone, but Jackie's mate was abusing her. Just like Christy's ex-husband was beating her. For years. Only Jackie didn't have anyone to step in and save her life the way Sebastian did for Christy. Jackie died at her mate's hands."

"Sweet Goddess, Matt. I'm sorry. I didn't know," she whispered, touched by the very real pain she saw in his expression.

"That's why, when Sebastian asked if I'd let Christy have my blood as her first meal, I agreed. He didn't know for sure that she was his One, yet. They hadn't been intimate. I think he suspected, and that's why he called me in before he knew for certain. Knowing the depth of their bond, I don't think he could've let her snack on my blood—and yes, have sex with me—if their bond was fully formed. As it was, I got caught up a bit in the echoes of their bond, and for a while there, I couldn't be too close to them. I went back to Las Vegas and stayed away for a good long time, waiting for the effect to fade."

Shifter blood was like a super fuel for vampires. It gave them some of the strength and attributes of the shifter they drank from for a period of time. If it was a first meal, the effect would last long into the vampire's formative years. By giving Christy his blood, Matt had given her the gift of his shifter strength, his cat agility, and even a bit of his ability to shapeshift.

Normally, shapeshifting was something that took many decades—even centuries—to master. But Christy was able to take other forms. Morgan had seen it herself, just once. She'd watched as Christy transformed from a small, white housecat, into her fully-clothed sexy vampiress form.

Morgan had been duly impressed at the time, but hadn't really stopped to wonder how a newly-made vampiress had been able to call on such skills. Now it all made sense.

"It was strictly a one-time deal," Matt went on. "Having felt just an echo of the bond between Christy and Sebastian..." He cleared his throat. "It's something really special. And I know they will never need me in that—or any other—capacity, ever again. They're it for each other, and that's the way it should be. For the record, while I respect Christy and have deep affection for her, I never loved her. My heart is free, unencumbered. And her heart belongs solely to her One. Sebastian. As it should be."

Was he protesting just a little too much? Morgan looked deep into his eyes when he turned his head to meet her gaze, and she realized that he was simply stating the truth. He was being a little emphatic—probably because he wanted her to understand what she hadn't given him a chance to say before. That was on her.

"What I'm trying to tell you is that what happened between me and Christy is something that I can never change. I wouldn't want to, even if I could. Because of my blood, she was able to face her past and find the courage inside her to confront her ex. She was able to fight back. Finally. And that's something every woman should have. Especially one who would have died at the hands of a man who should have protected her." His voice filled with emotion, and he looked away, breathing deeply before he spoke. "By the same token, it'll never happen again. I love Sebastian like a brother, and Christy will always hold a special place in my heart, but it's not the place a mate—or even a lover—would hold. It's more like she's my chance at redemption for not having been there to help Jackie."

The ice wall Morgan had built around her heart fractured at his words. She looked at him—his strong, chiseled face outlined against the dappled sunlight. There were depths to him she hadn't suspected. Pain and suffering had tempered him in ways she understood all too well. They had more in common than she'd thought. They'd both been through different kinds of hells with their families, only he'd come out mostly whole on the other side. Morgan knew there were large pieces of her soul missing, and nothing would ever fix that.

Still, she understood him so much better now. The ice wall began to fall away in chunks, first little ones and, then, really big ones, until nothing remained. She reached out to put her hand on his shoulder. A touch offering comfort.

"I'm sorry, Matt. I didn't know," she whispered.

But, then, she realized she was fibbing. She'd known about Christy and her ex. If she'd been a little more willing to see Matt as the hero he was rather than some sort of oversexed playboy, she could've pieced together most of the story herself. Her closed mind had refused to let her see.

Matt let out a breath and seemed to shake off his somber mood before he turned to meet her gaze. Then, he smiled that smile of his, and she fell a little under his spell, once more.

"So, what's the verdict? Do you forgive me? Can we start fresh or do you still want me run out of town on a rail?" His grin brought out the hint of a dimple. Now, that just wasn't playing fair.

She should really be asking for his forgiveness, but she had more than her fair share of pride. Instead, she just silently offered him her hand. He quirked his head at her gesture but took her hand, watching her closely.

"Hi, I'm Morgan, and I'd like to start over," she said quietly, wondering if she was doing the right thing in encouraging him. Like it or not, though, there was little else she could do at this point. He wasn't the villain she'd tried to make him out to be.

"Hi, Morgan. I'm Matt. Nice to meet you."

CHAPTER SIX

Goddess above, he was glad that conversation was over. And it had gone just about as well as Matt could've hoped. He really liked Morgan. Liked her enough to be thinking about bringing her home to meet his family. About letting the world know he'd found his mate.

He'd never really thought the mated life would be for him—settling down was fine for his brothers and other shifters, but Matt was more of a free spirit. He hadn't thought there'd be a match for him in the shifter world. Maybe a sexy vampire…

But no. He had suspected, almost from the moment they'd met, that Morgan was something special. He'd tried to ignore it. Had tried to run from it. Had allowed her to remain a mystery, so he wouldn't go tracking her down and claiming her.

It didn't work. Circumstance—or the Mother of All, if you believed in such things as fated mates—had thrown them together, again, and he was powerless to resist the pull of her, this time. Morgan made him want to leap out of bed, every morning, just so he could be near her. She made him want to be a better man, so he would be worthy of her. She made him want to claim her and be her mate, her friend, her lover, forevermore.

That was some heavy shit. Too heavy for a guy who usually liked to play it fast and loose, with few ties except the ones to his family.

"Well, this is about as exciting as watching grass grow," Matt quipped, wanting to work off some of his energy. "How about we prowl around a bit in our fur? We can get closer that way and use our cat senses to sniff around more." Plus, it would give him movement and the ability to shake off the emotions of the moment, which were running a little too high for his comfort.

Morgan looked skeptical but, then, relented. "Sounds good. I'll go over there and shift." She pointed to a cluster of bushes that would hide her from view. "No peeking," she admonished him with a wagging finger as she crept away toward the bushes.

Matt stifled a laugh. Most shifters were comfortable with nudity, but he had to remember Morgan hadn't spent much time with her own kind as an adult. From what he'd learned about her background—and it was spotty information, at best—she had been taken in by the Master vampire at a young age and raised away from shifters entirely. As a result, he had to cut her some slack if she wasn't all that familiar, or comfortable, with their ways.

Matt stripped and let his cat form come. It felt really good to go furry. He'd been stuck on two legs for more than a week, and his cat wanted to run. He leaned back on his paws and arched his back this way and that, getting a good long stretch for his reassembled spine. Mmm. That felt good.

While he was stretching, a petite cougar stepped daintily out from behind the bushes. Morgan.

His cat wanted to yowl in triumph. Here was a woman of his own kind, and she was as gorgeous to him in her fur as when she was in her human form. Her sleek coat begged for his touch. He wanted to lick her all over. And he wanted to run with her across the landscape, free and fast...and together.

He quickly quashed that wild idea—this was a time for

stealth—and promised himself that their time would come. When things were safe, he would take her out to the desert, and they would let their cat forms race across the wasteland. Later. After this problem was solved.

And to that end...

He waited for her to come up alongside him, and he bopped her cheek gently with his in greeting. She was smaller than him, but sleekly muscled. He'd bet she could really run, but it was their noses and stealth they needed to employ, right now. That and their silent paws.

Matt moved off through the low brush, heading on a circuitous route around the mine site. He knew of at least three different shafts that might allow entrance to the mine for someone his size, and a few dozen air shafts that would allow creatures smaller than a man inside. They could be useful listening posts if anyone was in the mine below. Their voices might carry up the sheer rock shafts.

They wove their way between trees, rocks and bushes, pausing here and there as they discovered scent trails and listened to what their senses could tell them about who had been this way recently. Matt paused when he picked up a scent he didn't expect.

He pawed the ground and caught Morgan's eye, asking her to double check his findings. She came over and sniffed delicately at the area he'd indicated and then sat back on her haunches, her quick motions indicating her surprise. She looked straight at him, blinking a few times before standing once more on all fours and bending to follow the trail of their unexpected visitor.

Matt tried to take note of the details of the scent. It was old, but there were layers to it...as if the person had come here several times over a period of days or even weeks. And there were other scents along with the one he recognized. These were strangers. Men. People Matt had never met or scented before.

But one thing was for sure. The primary scent they followed was female, and Matt had encountered it almost daily since coming to California to work on this project. There was little doubt in his mind that the scent trail they were following belonged to Irma, the ever-so-helpful receptionist at the winery's office.

The question was, what the hell had she been doing here? And who had she brought with her? Was it some kind of innocent thing or was there criminal activity going on? Or worse—magical activity?

Matt caught up with Morgan, nudging her to a stop. They had to go slow and be cautious. There was no telling what they would find at the end of this trail. Best case was nature-loving sightseers. Worse case was gun-toting criminals. And the *very* worst case scenario involved evil magic users with *Venifucus* ties.

Morgan moderated her steps, allowing Matt to keep pace with her. He watched her nose twitch as she followed the scent. Her cat face didn't allow a wide range of expression, but he knew how to read her eyes, which held both puzzlement and concern. He understood. If Irma was betraying them, how in the world had she gotten a job with Atticus in the first place?

Matt had to believe the vampire had precautions in place when he hired folks. Vampires—especially old ones like Atticus—had magical abilities that were unlike human mages or *were* skills. Atticus had to have put protective spells in place on his workplace and every area he owned. Matt had no doubt he vetted each and every employee with meticulous care.

So, how had Irma managed to fool him? How had she managed to fool Morgan and Matt? Shifters could tell a lot about a person by their scent. Lies had an odor all their own, but Matt hadn't sensed anything *off* about Irma's scent or her actions. She seemed more like a bubblehead than a master criminal or evil mage. Matt just didn't understand how they all could've missed something like that.

Unless she was just as innocent as they'd thought. Or…she was even more deceitful than any of them could have imagined. That thought made him shiver, and he hoped against hope that it turned out to be the former and definitely not the latter.

They reached a spot in the scent trail where the trees and shrubs thinned out, and the land sloped gently upward. Matt and Morgan crouched low, skirting around the open area until they came out on the other side and reacquired the scent. They could move a little faster now as the shrubbery was thicker. Matt paused at one point, alerting Morgan to a scrap of cloth that had snagged on a low branch. Farther along, he found more fibers. The interlopers hadn't come through this thicket unscathed.

He scented the coppery tang of blood ahead. More scratches by thorny branches? He slowed his pace, but Morgan sped up, and before he realized she'd gotten ahead of him, he heard her yowl in distress. It wasn't a loud sound, but it was definitely an "oh, shit" sound in cat form. Matt leapt after her, only to find the blood scent had grown much stronger.

In fact, there was a small slick of the red stuff, and poor Morgan had lost her footing and tumbled into it. He went straight to her, carefully avoiding the bloody spot. She looked miserable. Covered in muck and blood, she huddled pitifully, her head downcast, her eyes looking up at him as if seeking his help.

Matt shifted shape, staying close to the ground. He had to talk to her, and his human hands might be useful in figuring out what had happened here, even if he was bare-assed naked.

"Are you all right, sweetheart?" he asked in a low voice that wouldn't carry beyond them. "Anything hurt?" She shook her head, making a tiny cough that meant she was fine. Relief hit him hard.

To hide his reaction, he looked around the site. A very large snake had been killed and laid out a few feet away. He moved a little closer to investigate.

Everything about this kill wasn't right.

For one thing, this species of snake didn't naturally live in this area. And he could see from what was left of the body—which Morgan hadn't disturbed, thankfully—that it had been cut with a blade. Gutted. And the entrails spread in a particular pattern. It was arranged on the side of the hill, and its blood had poured downward to pool where Morgan had discovered it.

"This was done at least a day or two ago, and the forest scavengers haven't disturbed it." Matt frowned as he whispered his observations to Morgan. "That points toward enchantment," he thought aloud. "But why here?"

He looked around and spotted something just over Morgan's hunched shoulders. She turned her head, following the direction of his gaze.

"Son of a bitch," he whispered. "I didn't see that the last time I prowled through here." He crawled over to the opening in the rock that was almost totally covered with brush.

Sure enough, it was another entrance to the mine. One that everyone who had surveyed the area had missed, apparently. *Dammit.*

"This has to be where they're getting into the mine," he thought aloud. "Shit." He rested his elbows on his knees and thought.

Exercising caution, Matt looked over the site and wiped away any evidence that they'd come through. He even tried to doctor the area where Morgan had landed in the blood, turning over leaves and moving them to hide the evidence of her presence.

When all was as clear as he could make it, he looked at poor, blood-covered Morgan. "Let's get you cleaned up, sweetheart. We'll go to the pond, and you can take a dip to rid yourself of the blood, okay?"

Her eyes lit with approval of his idea, and he quickly shifted back to cougar form, motioning with his head for her to precede him. He followed after, making sure they left no evidence of their trail behind.

He caught up to her and nudged her toward the pond they had visited the day before with the human tour group. It was deep enough that she could submerge herself and swim around a bit. It also was fed by a small stream that kept the water fresh and flowing. A few fish and a turtle or two completed the idyllic spot. And it was in a safe area that wasn't easily seen from anywhere else on the property. They would be secure, for the moment, even if Irma and her friends returned.

He smelled the water ahead, and apparently, so did Morgan. She sped up, rushing into the pond as soon as she was close enough. Matt stood guard while she splashed around.

After a few minutes, the splashing sounds changed. Matt looked back to realize *she* had changed. Much to his surprise, she had shifted shape to her human form and was currently up to her neck in the pond, scrubbing at her hair and face.

"I don't want you to think I'm wimping out on you," Morgan said when she caught him watching her. "I'm a cat, you know. And I work with a bunch of vampires. I'm not usually skeeved out by a little blood." She paused to dunk her head again. "But there's something about the feel of this…" She trailed off as she scrubbed at her face. "It makes my skin crawl."

Matt shifted shape, so he could talk to her. He crouched down by the edge of the pond to rinse his hands. His paws had touched a bit of the blood, and he knew exactly what she meant.

"Blood magic," he said in a clipped voice, angry that someone would defile the land in such a way. Blood magic was the lowest of the low. The evilest of the evil.

Morgan paused in her splashing. He looked up to meet her gaze, and time stood still, for a moment.

"Are you sure?" It seemed like the entire forest held its breath, waiting for his answer.

"What else could it be? As far as I know there are no Burmese pythons roaming around Northern California on their own. The only way it could've gotten up here is if somebody brought it with them. And, judging by the amount of blood, they killed it right there." He paused, rinsing his hands again. "Did you see the pattern in the way it was laid out? It was very deliberate. Like a sacrifice or some kind of blood magic working. We should get the priestess to come up here and have a look, but I don't want to take the risk. It's obvious whoever killed the snake has been coming and going rather freely through here."

"Irma," Morgan said, her eyes narrowed. "I can't believe she would betray us."

"And, yet, there's no doubt it was her scent we both followed. Somehow, she's involved in all of this," Matt growled. "We should ask some of the Brotherhood to come up here and check it out, too. If anyone knows the different flavors of blood magic, it's a vampire."

"I'll call Marc when we get back to civilization," Morgan agreed. "The Master needs to know about this, first. He'll probably call a council once we report this."

"How does that work?" Matt asked, curious about her life and working arrangements. "I mean, when we first met, you were Marc's lawyer, but now, you're working for Atticus. Do you work for all of them, depending on their business needs?"

She tilted her head, rinsing her hair one more time. "Yeah, that's pretty much it. I go where they need me, and I keep an eye on most of the Brotherhood's business interests. Atticus needed me for this land deal, and he wants close supervision on the housing development, so I've been working out of his office at the vineyard, for a while now. This project is very important to him."

"To us, too. If I haven't said it before, I'm glad you're on the project. Your input has helped things move along a lot more smoothly than I expected."

She looked up at him, a pleased smile on her face. "Thanks."

Matt splashed his hands in the water some more,

scrubbing at the remnants of blood that felt vile. Now that he thought about it, Morgan was right. This stuff wasn't normal blood. It was tainted. Even he could feel it with only a small amount on his skin.

He was looking down at his hands when a wave of water hit him. Surprised, he looked up to find Morgan laughing and scooting away.

"Counselor, did you just splash me?" he asked in a mocking tone.

She giggled. "Now, would I do something like that?"

So, the kitty wanted to play. Matt grinned at her. This was the first truly playful impulse he'd seen from Morgan, and he liked it. She was far too serious all the time. He liked it when she laughed.

Hell, he just liked *her*. Period. She pushed all his buttons and then some. And he wanted to keep that smile on her face. Forever, if he could. He liked seeing her happy.

And he wanted more than anything to see her in pleasure, screaming his name. Moaning as he brought her to orgasm and made her his. For all time.

Whoa.

But, somehow, the thought didn't really stop the freight train of desire running through his system. No, it only pushed him forward. Egging him on until he dove, shallowly, headfirst into the pond.

He heard Morgan shriek with laughter a moment before the pure mountain water closed over his head. He swam underwater until he found her, grasping her around the waist as he broke the surface, her back to his front. He kept his hands around her waist, holding her in place.

"I've got you, now, counselor. There's no escaping my revenge," he teased.

She stilled against him, and he wished he could read the expression on her face. He felt the import of the moment. Something was going to happen here—and it was up to her which way this encounter would go.

"What if I don't want to escape?" she whispered, making

his heart race with excitement.

He pulled her back against him tightly, so she could feel his rising cock against her buttocks. When she didn't squirm away, his pulse began to pound. Was she giving him the go ahead? Was she willing to give them a chance?

He slid his hands over her torso under the water, walking them a little closer to shore where he could dig his feet more firmly into the slippery bottom of the rocky pond. He wouldn't take any chances with this special lady.

There was no need for words as she let him run his hands over her skin. When he moved to cup her breast, she moved into his touch, clearly welcoming it—welcoming him. He hadn't expected her to allow him any liberties this early in their relationship. Hell, he wasn't even sure she'd realized they were going to have a relationship, though he wanted her almost desperately, at this point.

But, now, things had changed. Thank the Goddess.

Matt turned her in his arms and dipped his head, lifting her up so he could kiss her. And she let him. No, more than that, she kissed him back. With interest.

He ran his hands over her body, then lifted her, moving her out of the water and up toward the bank. He set her on a large, flat rock, and she reclined, allowing him to do as he wished. And what he wished for most, at the moment, was to taste her...all over.

He lapped at her lips, leaving them only to trail kisses down her neck and over her chest, pausing at her nipples, licking and sucking until she moaned. And there it was, the sound he'd been dying to hear. It was one of many pleasure sounds he wanted to hear from her. He smiled, ticking that one off his mental list.

He went lower, his fingers leading the way, delving between her thighs. She spread for him, cooperating fully, stretching like a happy kitten beneath his touch. He touched her clit, circling gently, rubbing and stroking in the slick heat he found there, then he went lower, slipping inside with one finger, then two. He began a rhythm when she started moving her hips in what felt like a plea for action.

Kissing his way over her bellybutton and down lower, he licked her clit while his fingers slid in and out until she finally climaxed in spasms of pleasure. She called his name as she came. *Oh yeah.* That's another sound to check off on his list, though he wanted to hear her little sighs and moans as often as possible.

He moved back up her curvy form slowly, covering her softness with his own body until he could join their lips, once more. He kissed her with a lazy deliberateness, hoping to warm her up to going even farther.

And then, the earth moved.

No. Literally. It moved.

Matt drew away as Morgan sat up in alarm.

"Earthquake?" she asked, clearly still a little fuzzy from pleasure.

"A small tremor, at least," Matt confirmed as the earth stilled.

The forest had gone completely quiet around them. If they hadn't been so distracted a few minutes ago, they probably would have realized the quake was coming by the silence of the forest creatures.

"We'd better go," Matt said reluctantly. The romantic mood had been broken by the very real and disturbing evidence of seismic activity that could mean something simple...or much more sinister. They didn't really have time to pursue their passion, right now. It was becoming clear that there was a real problem in this forest and, especially, underground.

They shapeshifted and loped quickly back to where they'd left their clothes, keeping alert to the possibility of intruders. Dressing with little discussion, Matt sent off a quick text message to Sebastian, outlining what they'd found.

Morgan finished dressing and turned to him. "So, what do you think?"

"I texted what we know to Sebastian. He won't get the message 'til tonight when he rises, but at least someone will know what we're up to."

Morgan nodded. "Good idea. I'll do the same with Atticus and Marc." She was already reaching for her cell phone, beginning to tick away at the touch screen.

"I think we'd better go into the mine and see what we can find out from the inside. It's clear someone's been getting in there. Irma and a few friends, at least." He gave a snort of annoyance. "I want to see if we can track their path down below and figure out what they've been up to. The tremor we just felt is a bit too much of a coincidence for me not to look into it."

"You think they caused it, somehow?" She was giving voice to what they both were thinking. She didn't really wait for an answer. "Do you think it's safe? They wouldn't collapse the mine, would they?"

Matt thought about that, for a moment. "If they're working magic down there, they won't want to be caught in it. Stands to reason, they wouldn't be trying to deliberately collapse the mine. They probably have some larger goal in mind." He didn't like the bigger possibilities. "The real question in my mind is whether the tremor was a byproduct of whatever they were doing, or are they actually trying to call an earthquake?"

CHAPTER SEVEN

Morgan was shocked by the idea that someone would deliberately try to trigger an earthquake. In this part of the world, where small tremors were common, medium ones frequent, and big ones not unheard of, there was every possibility that magic could call forth something truly devastating from the earth.

"Why would they want to do that?" she asked, aghast as the possibilities presented themselves in her mind.

"At least two separate *Venifucus* mages—in Iceland and again, in Washington state—tried to harness the power of a volcano in recent months to fracture the veil between our mortal realm and the place where Elspeth is. They want to bring her back. We know that. Perhaps, there's some way to use the energy released in a catastrophic earthquake for the same ends?"

"Sweet Mother of All," she whispered.

"Which is why I need to get in there and see what I can find out before that little tremor we felt possibly turns into something much bigger." Matt looked determined, but Morgan felt the same.

"I'm going with you," she announced, knowing he would argue but not willing to let him leave her behind.

"Morgan—" Whatever he would have said was interrupted

by another tremor, this one a little bit stronger.

She swayed on her feet, reaching out to take Matt's hand as he offered it to her. They clung to each other's arms as the earth beneath them moved uncontrollably, for a few moments.

When it subsided, she was breathing hard, fear of the possible danger making her heart race. But she wouldn't let that stop her. Something was wrong here, and they needed to find out as much as they could before anything else happened.

"I'm not arguing with you, Matt, but we both need to go in there. At the very least, by two of us going in, we double the odds of at least one of us getting out again in time to tell the Brotherhood—and your people, too—whatever we learn."

Matt looked skeptical. "I don't like your math, sweetheart. You should go back to the office and be ready to call in the troops once I find out exactly what's going on here. I can get backup in a half hour—maybe less. I'll call in some of the work crews."

"Do you really want to blow any advantage we have?" she asked shrewdly. "It's likely Irma, and whoever has been going down into the mine with her, doesn't know we're on to them. But, if you call in a Pack of shifters to traipse all over these woods, they'll figure it out pretty quick. We need to act now. With stealth."

Matt cursed as he let go of her arms. He turned and moved a few paces away from her, then spun back, clearly agitated.

"I'm probably going to regret this," he muttered, then walked right up to her, facing her. "All right. You win. Let's go."

Morgan tried hard not to smile in triumph. But then, she thought about the danger of what they were about to do, and any amusement vanished.

He started to walk silently through the trees, out of their hiding spot. She noted how he was careful to erase any small evidence of their presence, and she did the same. Matt was better in the wild, but she was a shifter, and she learned fast.

"Where are we going?" she asked in a quiet voice that wouldn't carry past the two of them.

"Alternate entrance near the tunnel I think they're using," he said in the same tone. "I have a good idea of the layout of the mine, but that entrance we spotted earlier isn't on any of the maps. Still, I have a notion of where that entrance connects with the rest of the tunnels and shafts. I can get us close enough through this other way in that we can approach quietly through the tunnels. Better chance of finding them this way, and less possibility of being caught at it."

She followed his lead, glad she'd packed light for a day she knew would probably require shapeshifting at some point. All she had with her was what she could carry in her pockets. She had lived the life of a city cat for far too many years to be comfortable trekking long distances through the woods in her human form.

While she had shifter stamina and strength no matter what form she wore, her cat was better able to cope with the forest. But she couldn't shapeshift, at the moment, so her two aching feet did their best to keep up with Wilderness Guide Matt on what was beginning to feel like a forced march through far too many trees with pointy, sharp edges that wanted to snag her clothes, her hair, and her skin.

In fact, Matt had to stop twice to remove bits of her hair from overly aggressive branches. After the second time, she was more careful to remove any bits of fiber, hair or even blood from the small scratch on her arm, from the thorny offenders. It was clear Matt didn't want to leave even the minutest trace of their passing and she understood his caution. They were dealing with magic users that were probably in league with the *Venifucus*. Such evil creatures would be hard to sneak up on, but that was exactly what she and Matt were proposing to do.

Goddess help them.

Still, there was nobody else. They had to find out as much

as they could about what was going on below ground, and they had to do it now. Before it escalated into something they might not be able to stop.

Matt led her to a small entrance that was known but disused. In fact, they had to do a little breaking and entering to get in. Matt pried just enough boards away for them to scramble through, then did his best to replace them from the inside, so it wouldn't be obvious they had been moved.

The farther they moved into the tunnel, the darker it became. Morgan relied on her cat's superior vision, but eventually, even that didn't help much in the pitch black of the underground tunnel system. A shiver ran down her spine when the light failed completely as they turned a sharp bend in the tunnel.

Matt stopped in front of her, and she walked into his back. He turned and steadied her, moving close to whisper near her ear as he took her hand. His touch was incredibly reassuring.

"We'll go slow. There are air shafts all over the place that let in a little light, here and there. I've been into this part of the mine before, and the truly pitch black places don't last long. I don't want to chance using a light until we know where the bad guys are, but I know where I'm going. Don't worry."

Not wanting to chance speaking too loudly, she nodded against his cheek and squeezed his hand. She was already working hard to memorize every turn they took, so she would have a chance of getting out again if they, somehow, got separated.

"Good girl," he said, placing a gentle kiss on her temple before moving back. But he didn't go far. He kept hold of her hand and stayed at her side.

Around the next turning in the tunnel, she saw the quality of the dark change. There was a dim glow up ahead, and as they drew closer, she saw it was one of the air shafts Matt had mentioned. It let in enough of the daylight that she could see again, and she felt relieved. As long as she knew those little air shafts were around, she wouldn't freak out too much in the pitch black spots.

They passed four more air shafts before her ears began to pick up strange sounds coming from below. Matt paused, his steps slowing even more as they began their stealthy approach to whatever was making those eerie sounds.

It sounded like mumbling at first, but as they got closer, the sheer rock faces carried the echoes of strange words to them. Words that felt dirty in a sinister way, even as they bounced off the rocks and went past them.

Chanting. A deep voice chanting evil words.

Yeah, that couldn't be good.

The chanting stopped long before they saw the glimmer of red growing brighter as they moved closer. Each twist in the tunnel brought them closer to the source of the red light, and the people who were bathed in its glow.

The deep voice was replaced by one she knew well. Irma was chanting now. Her voice louder and more distinct, ringing against the stone walls as Matt and Morgan walked deeper into the mine.

Morgan picked up on the hum of electricity through the very old wires that had been strung along the ceiling of the shaft. There was lighting in some parts of the mine, and it became apparent that Irma and her friends were using one of the strings of lights. Probably the section closest to the hidden entrance they had used to get in.

Humans didn't have the best night vision. They'd need lights to see where they were going. Especially this deep down into the mine. The pressure in her ears told Morgan all she needed to know about how deep into the earth they had travelled on their winding, downward trek. This had to be one of the deepest parts of the mine, if not *the* deepest.

If these *Venifucus* jerks were trying to cause an earthquake, it made sense they'd want to be as deep into the earth as possible. Damn them.

The red glow grew brighter, turning into an orangey-yellow as they turned another corner. Another twist took them to a bare light bulb hanging forlornly at the end of the wire in the ceiling. Nobody was near it.

The floor was still sloping sharply downward. If what Morgan suspected was true, Irma and company would be at the lowest point in the mine. From the maps she had seen, she knew there was a section at the lowest point that had been used to collect the ore before shipping it back up by pony cart in the oldest days of the mine. It was a wide, open area about twelve feet across and forty feet long. There were little storage bays and offshoots all along the tunnel, if she recalled correctly. Maybe they could hide in one of those and observe whatever Irma and her pals were doing.

As they neared, it seemed Matt was thinking along the same lines. He moved low and silently, crouching as he ducked into one of the side rooms. It was open at the back, and she soon discovered there was a small passageway between the storage areas that they could exploit to get closer to where Irma was still chanting.

Matt led the way, moving with the utmost care until they were in a storage cubby was at an oblique angle to the center part of the chamber. Morgan could just see the back of a rather wide man, who wore a red robe that had a sheen to it like velvet or some kind of thick satin. There was writing around the hem in a broad border, but the symbols were arcane. Not something she had ever seen before. And not necessarily something she ever wanted to see again.

Just looking at the symbols made her feel queasy. No doubt, they were evil magical glyphs of some kind. Power flowed around the man, and she could almost see a sort of glowing bubble around him, reaching out to meet similar spheres around the other two people.

She could just barely see the other two. One was a tall, thin fellow with a black robe on. It too, had the band of symbols running around the hem. And then, she saw Irma. She was in profile, moving in and out of visual range as she swayed and chanted. She was wearing a red robe, like the first man, and it had those evil glyphs running up and down the front in two, parallel rows and around the edges of her sleeves.

The spheres of power radiated out from each one of them and overlapped, joining together where they met to encase the trio in some kind of force field. Morgan noted the ring that had been laid out on the floor, as well. They were standing in some sort of magical circle they had created. She didn't know too much about magic, but she knew why many magic users cast circles. They were meant to keep things in, or out.

In this case, the ring, along with the bubbles of power, were probably meant to keep the roof from falling in on their heads while they did their evil work. And Morgan knew, without a doubt, that their aim was to cause an earthquake because just as another, even larger tremor struck, Irma cried out in delight, smiling even as the earth shook with them in it.

The mages were protected, but Matt and Morgan weren't within the realm of their magical influence. And they were at the epicenter of the quake.

Matt grabbed her hand and began to run. Noise didn't matter so much with the earth groaning around them, but they were shifters and could run silently in either of their forms. They backtracked through the tunnel system and made it to an area much higher in the mountain as rocks and debris clattered down around them.

Morgan thought they'd make it out, but just as they reached the third air shaft, disaster struck.

"Shit!" Matt cursed quietly as the rumble of thousands of pounds of rock echoed off the walls, roaring past them. The tunnel collapsed behind them as they ran.

They turned a corner, just under the little air shaft that let in light, and came to a screeching halt. The way was blocked by a cave-in that must've happened only moments before.

"We're trapped," she whispered over the roar of rock.

Matt spun her into his arms as the thunder of the collapse galloped toward them. Would the roof fall in on them, crushing them to death? Or would they simply be trapped below ground with no way to get out?

Either option scared the shit out of her. Morgan sent a prayer up to the Goddess while Matt used his hard body to shield her from the rocks shaking loose from above. He crouched against the side of the tunnel, directly below the air shaft, holding her close and using his own body to protect her.

She lifted the neck of her T-shirt over her nose and mouth to try to filter out some of the dust and helped Matt do the same. They huddled together like that for what felt like hours, but were probably only a few minutes before the noise and fury of the earth subsided.

The dust took much longer to settle, but when Morgan could breathe freely again, she scented the coppery tang of blood. Matt's blood.

"You're hurt," she said in a shaky voice. It was the best she could manage under the circumstances.

"Some of those rocks were sharp," he joked.

"Let me up so I can see," she demanded, worried for him.

He moved gingerly, which spoke volumes to her about his injuries. She stood and examined him from head to toe. He had a gash on the back of his shoulder that was already beginning to scab over and numerous small cuts on his hands and forearms.

"Nothing too serious that I can see," she reported, feeling relieved. "Are you sure nothing else is wrong?"

"You mean besides being trapped down here?" he quipped, hands on hips, looking around at the small space they found themselves in.

She told herself to be calm. Hysteria wouldn't help in this situation, but boy, did she want to scream. Or break down and cry. Luckily, she didn't do either. But she did reach out to grip Matt's hand. He was her lifeline. Her sanity.

He pulled her back into his arms, apparently sensing how close she was to the edge. He soothed her, running his hands down her back and rocking her gently, for a few moments.

"It'll be okay. We're still alive, and our friends know where we were headed. They'll send help. Somebody will find us, if we don't manage to find a way out ourselves in the next few hours. We have air and light. We'll get through this," he crooned. "You'll see."

"Those bastard mages probably got out the other way. I bet they cast protections on their escape route," she said, growing angry. Anger was much better than hysteria.

"Yeah, you're probably right. They're just practicing, after all. The big event still hasn't happened yet," he told her.

Suddenly, she realized what he meant. These tremors were just that—weak tremors that had been growing in magnitude. It was a build-up. A prelude to something much worse and much, much bigger.

"It would have to be pretty strong to pierce the veil between worlds, from what I've heard," Matt continued. "A big earthquake might do it, but I don't think these little tremors are enough, yet. They're still working toward the big one. Which means..." he paused, letting her go as he began to survey the small chamber that had been created by the quake once more, "...we still have time to stop them."

Morgan remembered her cell phone and quickly checked it. The signal strength was low, but it did have signal. The only problem was her battery. It was running low.

Matt saw what she was doing and reached into his pocket, but the phone he pulled out was seriously damaged. The glass screen was shattered, and it wouldn't even power on.

"So much for that," he grumbled. "What about yours?" She filled him in on her battery issue, and he frowned. "Better save it for tonight after the vamps rise. We can use the rest of the day to try to get ourselves out, and if we haven't made a dent in this rock pile by nightfall, we can call Marc and get the cavalry—if they haven't already figured out we need help. The messages we left before we came in here ought to alert them. Especially when we don't check in as promised."

"Yes," she said, powering down the phone and putting it away. "You're right, of course." She was comforted by his positive outlook, even if she was still freaked out by being trapped.

"But first…" Matt walked over to her and took her into his arms again. "We both need to calm down. I need a few more minutes for my shoulder to heal, and you need a hug. Come to think of it, I need a hug too." He smiled as he hugged her close, leaning back against the wall of the tunnel.

He held her in the near-silence, for long moments, the only sound that of their breathing and the occasional slide of pebbles as the newly formed piles of rock settled. His arms were so very comforting. So strong. So able. Just like him.

Matt was everything she dreamed of in a man, when she allowed herself to fantasize about a perfect world where a mate wouldn't try to rule her life and keep her down. She hadn't thought a relationship like that was possible. She thought it the stuff of fairytales, used to beguile women into accepting the yoke of mating.

But everything she'd learned of Matt and his Clan… She was changing her mind. Maybe the Redstones really were different. Maybe her home Clan had been warped. Old fashioned. Backward. It was entirely possible. Until Morgan had met Marc LaTour, she hadn't even attended school regularly.

Marc had seen to it that she received the finest education money could buy. And he'd arranged for tutors, at first, to get her up to speed with the rest of her age group. She'd had private tutors in everything from math to deportment. She'd had to learn how to interact with humans and Others. She'd had to learn how to speak properly and even how to read.

But Marc had helped her. He'd kept track of her progress and encouraged her until she was able to join a normal class of human children and not stand out. Marc had taught her how to hide her differences from the humans. How to blend in and walk among them without fear. He'd been her mentor and her guide, and she'd come to trust that bloodletters, at least, didn't devalue women.

Matt had been showing her that his Clan felt the same. The women Morgan had met and learned about from the Redstone Clan were confident and out here in the world, doing things. Working. In charge.

Seeing that had gone a long way toward changing Morgan's attitude about the Redstone Clan—and its local representative. His gentleness and protective nature also impressed her, and his strong arms and willingness to treat her as an equal went the rest of the way toward earning her respect.

And now, she was stuck in a deep, dark hole with him. And yet...somehow...when he held her as he was doing, she wasn't afraid. She sensed his confidence in their ability to get out of this alive, and it reassured her.

She felt his heart beating against her cheek and the strength of his arms around her shoulders. She smelled his warm, masculine scent and heard the steady beat of his breath. He wasn't alarmed, and so, she wasn't either. He gave that gift to her. The gift of calm...and of hope.

And earlier that day, he'd given her the most amazing climax of her life.

Her thoughts turned decidedly naughty as her blood heated. She moved her hands on his back and around his torso, reaching downward. It was time. Time to seal this deal and feed the hunger that had been building inside her since the moment they'd first met.

"Matt?" she whispered, raising her head, seeking his lips in the dim light.

He didn't disappoint her. He lowered his head and touched his mouth to hers, allowing her to lead the way, to take possession of his lips, then delve inside, taking the kiss deeper. She wanted it all, and she told him so without words, in the most delicious way possible.

She felt the rumble in his chest before the purr came to life in the quiet dark. She wasn't afraid of it now. It was good and right. And she discovered an answering vibration in her own chest. Only Matt had ever made her purr, and she was through fighting it.

The world might go to hell in an hour, or a day, or a week, but she wanted this moment with him. The man who pleased both her beast and herself. The man who seemed like her perfect match in every way.

Was he too good to be true? Only time would tell. But for now, she wanted him. She wanted to be with him and belong to him and have him belong to her.

She reached for his shirt, pulling it out from his pants. He helped, ridding himself of his clothing, then starting in on hers. She noted absently that he made a little pile of the discarded clothing right next to them. Sure enough, when they were both naked, he eased her down onto the pile of fabric.

"Sorry we don't have a featherbed and soft sheets. I dreamed of this moment, and I never expected—" Matt said in a rush as his breathing escalated. They were both excited and ready for more, but it was sweet of him to apologize for something beyond his control. She stopped his words by laying one finger over his lips.

"It's all right. It's perfect, Matt. It's how it was meant to be, and I don't need anything but you right now." He made her breath catch by licking her finger then sucking it into his mouth, holding her gaze all the while. "And I do mean *right* now," she added in a whispery, amused voice.

He smiled and let her finger go, swooping in to catch her lips. She let him lead the dance, for a little while, but then, her cat felt like asserting itself, and Matt let her roll him beneath her as she straddled him.

There was no time for preliminaries. No time for finesse or drawn out foreplay. The pounding need inside her demanded immediate action. No more waiting. No more uncertainty. It was time. Long past time.

Morgan reached between them and guided him into her body, feeling the stretch and burn as she took him. He was larger than anyone she'd been with before. Then again, she'd never been with a shifter before. Up 'til now, her only experience was with human men who had never known her true nature. It was no wonder none of those relationships had lasted. If she couldn't be herself with her lover, what was the point?

But she could give Matt all she was and then some. He could take it. He would answer her wild nature with his own. They could be wild together and unleash the cats within. In fact, it was inevitable.

Morgan sank down on him, taking him fully as her hands changed just a little bit, small claws emerging in place of her fingernails. She noticed Matt's hands had done the same. His claws weren't sharp enough to puncture her skin, but she felt the indentation of all ten digits in the soft flesh around her hips as he guided her motion.

She began to move, drawing her own claws down his chest, not hurting, but letting the cat inside her come out to play. Matt growled, his eyes half-lidded in pleasure as he looked up at her.

"Do that again," he told her in clear approval. She did it again, and he jerked slightly under her body. Yeah, he really liked that.

She wanted to explore that sensation further, but her body needed to move, to take him and ride him until they both screamed out in passion. Almost without conscious volition, her hips began a steady rhythm, her inner muscles squeezing and releasing as his hips thrust upward into her. The muscles in her thighs strained, as did his. She threw back her head as pleasure reached for her, and braced her hands on his thighs behind her.

Then, Matt reached up and ran his claws lightly over the sensitive skin of her breasts, her abdomen, the small of her back, down her thigh and all over. Each erogenous zone. Places she hadn't even known could be so sensitive. He discovered each one and made her squeak and moan as he drew every ounce of response from her body.

She keened as a wave of climax hit her, stopping her motion while her body seized up. But Matt wasn't still. He flipped her and put her beneath him on the pile of clothes, arranging her body to suit him as he took over, pounding home into her tight sheath, pushing her toward another, even higher, level of pleasure.

"Matt!" she cried out his name as she went farther than she'd ever gone before. There was an element of fear in their passion. Like she wasn't quite sure she could survive the coming explosion. But Matt was with her. He was her guide and her lover. He would see her through the disintegration and reassembly on the other side. She trusted him.

And there it was. She trusted him.

That moment of startling clarity erupted into the most amazing experience of her life. There was no Morgan in that moment of pure bliss. There was no Matt. No mountain on top of them and no evil in the world. There was only pleasure. The pure, good, blessed pleasure of being with the one who was meant for you.

Mate. Matthew Redstone was her mate.

She didn't really know all that entailed. She'd lived on the fringes of shifter society for most of her life. But, if the Goddess willed it, they might still have time to figure this all out.

For now, it was enough to know that she had found her One, like the bloodletters she so admired. For each soul, there was one perfect match. Something inside her soul clicked with Matt, and she knew in her heart of hearts that he was it for her.

Goddess help them.

CHAPTER EIGHT

Matt had claimed his mate. Dear Goddess, he had finally found her and claimed her. He was truly blessed. He'd known she was his for a while, and now, Morgan knew it too, beyond the shadow of a doubt.

Matt had suspected Morgan might be the one when they first met all those months ago, but her skittishness and his wandering lifestyle had made it hard for him to pin her down. There was something oddly amusing about the fact that it had taken an earthquake and getting buried alive to get them together. It would be a story to tell their grandchildren. If they made it that far.

For now, it was enough to have her in his arms, and have the knowledge in his heart that she was the one meant for him. Mating was serious business, and Matt knew exactly how lucky he was to have found his match. She'd led him a merry chase, but in the end, she had come to him, and he would do everything in his power to make certain that she never regretted her decision in the years to come—if they had that long. And he'd do all he could to make sure they had the time together to have cubs and grow old and do all the things he wanted to do with her.

Daydreams spun through his mind as they lay together in the aftermath of the most magical experience of his life. They had both purred there, for a while, in the afterglow.

Never had he dreamed he would find a woman so perfectly matched to him. She was a cougar, which was something he hadn't taken for granted, seeing as how two of his brothers had mated with non-shifters. Matt hadn't known what to expect, really. He'd been open to any possibility the Mother of All might send his way, but once he'd met Morgan, he'd found it hard to get her out of his mind.

No wonder. She was his mate!

He must have recognized their connection on some basic level, but now, he had irrefutable evidence that even she couldn't deny. He squeezed her closer and bent to kiss the top of her head, which rested against his chest. Exactly where she belonged.

With him. Next to him. On top of him, or under him. As long as she was with him, he'd be a happy man for the rest of his life. However long, or short that turned out to be.

"Feels like the mountain has quieted. Maybe the mages gave up and went home," he mused, stroking her hair. He wanted to say so much more, but he knew he'd have to tread lightly with his skittish mate. She would have to come to him, but he was a patient man. He could wait as long as she needed. He loved her enough to give her all the room she needed to be comfortable with this. With *them*.

"We should be so lucky." She rested her hand over his heart, which now beat only for her. "I guess it's okay to tell you now that I'm a little freaked out by being trapped in tiny spaces."

A tremor ran through her body as she said the words, and he hugged her closer, soothing her.

"Sweetheart, you can tell me anything. Anytime. I would never betray your trust, and I won't think less of you for admitting to being less than the superhero lawyer everyone else sees when they look at you." He smiled at her when she met his gaze, resting her chin against his chest. "You're kinda scary, you know? In a really hot, powerful, lady lawyerly way," he was quick to clarify when her eyes narrowed. "And I really admire that about you. It's totally hot. But knowing that you suffer from some of the same frailties as the rest of us mere mortals makes you a bit more approachable. And it makes me want to touch you, and squeeze you, and do all sorts of wicked, delicious things with you."

She smiled at him, and her body seemed to relax against him, once more. "You do have a way with words when you get going, Redstone."

"I try, counselor. I try." He stroked her hair back from her face, gazing deep into her eyes. "So, why the fear of enclosed spaces? Can you tell me about it?"

She turned away and moved so that her cheek was against his chest again and she was draped over him. It was probably easier for her to talk about her fears if she didn't have to look at him, he realized, though he wanted so much to take any burdens of uncertainty off her fragile shoulders. He'd do anything for her. He'd fight battles. He'd cross oceans. He'd face hell itself to keep her safe.

Whoa. He knew he was probably being a little over-dramatic, but he cut himself some slack seeing as how he'd just claimed his mate. That sort of thing was bound to bring up all sorts of epic feelings in a guy.

"I've never told anyone about it," she whispered after a long pause. "My father used to lock me in a closet if I did something bad. I hated it."

Matt read between the lines. She didn't just hate the closet. She hated the man who had put her in it. And Morgan, being a decent sort of person, probably had a lot of guilt over the idea of hating her own flesh and blood. But Matt had seen this before, in some of the folks who sought refuge with the Redstone Clan. Not all shifters were nice people. Some folks, Matt had decided, should just never be parents.

"I hear you, Morgan," Matt said gently, wanting to sooth her and just be there for her. He rubbed her arms and held her close, speaking in non-verbal ways of his love and support. "That can't have been easy. And it explains a bit more about why you had such a bad impression of the shifter community."

"I've learned a lot since your people have come here. Just in the past couple of days, I've gotten to see Redstone Clan members in action, and if they're anything to go by, my home Clan was nothing like what it should have been—what your people have." She was quiet for a moment, but Matt sensed she still had more to say. "That closet actually saved my life, so I guess I should be thankful for it now."

Matt grew concerned, sensing, somehow, what she might tell him next would be just awful. Did he really want to know? Yeah, he had to know. He wanted to know every hurt his beautiful mate had suffered so he could understand her and help her...and hunt down every last bastard who had hurt her and slay them.

"What happened, Morgan?" he asked quietly, prompting her, but trying not to pressure her. He carefully kept his tone as neutral and comforting as possible.

"They came in the middle of the night. I never saw who it was, but someone—a group of someones—came through the house and shot every member of my family." Her tone was weary. Defeated.

But Matt didn't understand. Shifters were strong. Mere bullets couldn't keep them down for long.

"Were they silver bullets?" he asked, still in that same, careful tone.

"Worse," she replied. "Tranquilizers. Really strong ones. I heard the *fwap-fwap-fwap* as the rounds left the rifles. Multiple rounds of fast-acting tranqs. That's what I think happened, anyway. I could scent the chemicals, and they were heady. I couldn't actually see anything because—as usual—I was locked in the hidden closet." She sighed and seemed to be calmer as she related the story. "I heard a lot of banging and dragging sounds as they took my family out of the house, none too gently. I didn't dare breathe. I knew, if they realized I was still there, they'd get me too." Her hand on his chest clenched into a fist as she continued to tell her tale in broken segments.

"You must have been very brave," Matt commented.

"Scared spitless," she quipped, giving a delicate snort. "Then, about an hour later, they started screaming. One by one, I heard the screams of my family. My mother, my father, my aunts and uncles. I was the only cub, thank goodness. I guess the folks who killed the adults of my family didn't realize there had been any young." Matt placed his hand over her fist, grateful when she uncurled her tight fingers and laced them with his before she went on. "I must have slept at some point after the noise stopped. I was stuck in that closet and couldn't get out. I was too scared what might be outside if I managed to break out. So I stayed there, silent and scared, for the rest of that day. That night, Marc came. He had been in the area, for a while. I know I'd heard my father curse the bloodletter that lived up the hill. We had been alone in the swamp before then. There was a house—a mansion, really— up on the hill, and at one time, there had been a plantation, but the house had been empty for years, and our Clan expanded farther into the swamp, seeking areas away from the humans who were encroaching on our lands."

Her words drifted off, and Matt let her go at her own pace while he reflected on what she was telling him. What she'd been through was even more horrific than he'd expected. She was a strong woman to have come through that and made so much of herself. And now Matt finally understood a little bit more about why she was so close with the Master vampire.

"Marc had noticed something off in the swamp, the night before, but the attackers had come close to dawn, and Marc had to go to ground. The following night, he came to investigate, and he sensed me in the closet and let me out. I was so scared, at first. I thought he was going to kill me too, but he didn't. He saved me. He protected me. He got me out of there and made sure I didn't see the horror of what they'd done to my family. From that night until this one, Marc has been my protector, my savior, my dear friend. He even moved out of the house on the hill and came here, because he didn't think it was good for me to be in that environment where so much had taken place. He brought us to California and made a fresh start here. Soon after, he stepped into the role of Master, and everything fell into place for him…and for me. He paid for my education, and I went to the finest schools in California. He kept me close, but also allowed me to grow and learn and spread my wings as far as I was willing to go. And, when you showed up last year…he nudged me into meeting you."

She looked up at him again, her gaze full of wonder that made Matt's heart fill with hope.

"You were the first shifter I'd met since leaving Florida," she admitted. "I didn't want to. I never wanted anything to do with shifters ever again after getting out of that closet, but Marc knew I'd need to learn more about my own kind, eventually." She squeezed his hand. "I'm glad you were my first re-introduction to shifters. And I'm glad you turned out to be so much different than everything I remembered and feared."

The moment was golden. Full of emotion and portent.

"I'm glad too, Morgan," Matt admitted in a solemn tone. "You intrigued me from the moment I scented you."

She blushed. He couldn't help himself—he rose up so that they were sitting on the pile of discarded clothing and took her into his arms and kissed her. It was a kiss of acceptance and caring, of tenderness and joy, of loneliness banished and terror forgotten.

When they came up for air, the faint light in their little cavern was decidedly dimmer.

"Night is falling. Our cavalry may arrive soon," Matt said with a slight grin.

"I sincerely hope so." Morgan shivered, a little of her fear entering her gaze as she remembered where they were.

"I promise you, Morgan…" Matt stilled to make her a solemn vow. "If it's the last thing I ever do, I'll get you out of here." He smiled, breaking the tension, a heartbeat later, before she could get scared. "But it won't come to that. We haven't even tried digging yet, and our friends know where we were headed. Marc has moved for you before. You have to believe he'll move this little bit of dust and rock to get you out of here. Have faith, sweetheart. You're part of a bigger family now. One that protects its own. We'll be out of here lickity-split."

She looked at him doubtfully but seemed to take heart from his words, finally drawing away and sorting through the messy pile of clothes to find her bra. Matt was sorry to see her getting dressed, but he also knew they should probably try digging a bit. There might not be all that much between them and the outer portion of the tunnel. But digging naked wasn't recommended. For one thing, the rocks were sharp in places. For another, there was a lot of dust that would mix with sweat to form uncomfortable mud. *No, thank you.*

Matt reluctantly followed Morgan as she stood and helped her sort out her clothes, stealing kisses in exchange for her garments as he handed them to her. He pulled on his shorts and pants, then his shirt, glad he'd packed a few things in his cargo pockets. He fished out a granola bar and handed it to her.

"Nibble on this while I take a look at what we've got. There might be some unstable sections we should avoid."

Morgan looked like she wanted to argue, for a moment, but then she took the granola bar and shrugged. "You'd know more about that sort of thing than I do, seeing as how you build things for a living."

Matt smiled and leaned down to give her a quick kiss. "Thanks for the vote of confidence. For the record, that's the reason I wanted you to stay back here while I checked things out. I'm familiar with the signs of stable rock and what constitutes a dangerous situation. My goal here is keeping you safe, not keeping you in a corner. Okay?" He waited until she nodded before moving cautiously away, closer to the debris zone.

The light was dimming quickly now as night began to creep across the landscape up top. Matt had a small penlight in his pocket, which he used to examine the pile of rocks and dirt that blocked their path.

"This doesn't look too bad, actually," he reported as he continued his inspection. "I think it's safe enough if we dig in line with this wall." He ran his hands over the layer of loose dirt, shaking some loose. "With any luck, there won't be too much damage to the tunnel past this point, and we won't have far to dig. Plus, our friends will probably be digging from the other side as soon as we let them know exactly where we are."

Morgan reached for her phone, but didn't power on. "It's not really dark yet," she stated. "Best wait until full dark so I'm sure Marc is awake." She put the phone back into her pocket and moved closer to Matt, reaching out to brush away some of the dirt near the low ceiling of the tunnel.

"We'll go slow, at first, just to be sure everything is stable," Matt cautioned, joining her, reaching for the highest point and working downward.

They worked together for at least a half hour and had dug several feet into the debris pile. They hadn't broken through to the other side, yet, but Morgan felt better that at least they were making some kind of progress. Sitting around feeling helpless wasn't high on her list of favorite things to do.

She was still freaking out at being confined, but Matt's presence helped. In fact, when he'd been making love to her, she hadn't realized they were trapped, at all. Matt had a way of narrowing her focus to just the two of them. Together.

It was a heady thought. She wondered if their joining had been as epic for him as it had been for her. She had zero experience of shifter lovemaking, but even so, she thought Matt must be pretty special, even among shifters. He had shown her a fiery passion she hadn't known was inside her. He'd introduced her to hungers she hadn't known she possessed. And she was very much afraid that he'd ruined her for anyone else, ever again.

She wanted only him. Her inner cat stood up and yowled in agreement. It had a single-minded determination where

Matt Redstone was concerned. Her cat wanted him for all time. She wanted him as her mate.

The absurdity of that thought was almost enough to get her mind off her fear of being trapped down here in this hole. Almost.

A nearly crippling anxiety crept in, and she did her best to hide it from Matt, but she knew he knew. How could he not, after she'd shared that shameful bit of her past with him. This small chamber in what had once been a tunnel brought back all kinds of trauma from her childhood. She was just barely holding herself together, but Matt's gentle touches and pats on her shoulder—his reminders that she wasn't alone down here—helped considerably.

The other thing that helped was prayer. As she worked, Morgan kept up a steady litany of prayers to the Mother of All, asking for her guidance and help. Morgan wasn't ashamed to admit she might even have begged for assistance from the Goddess who was known to sometimes intervene directly in the lives of those who worshipped Her.

Morgan truly didn't expect a response to her prayers, but when the wall of dirt in front of her began to glow, she stopped digging and just stared. It was Matt who pulled her out of the way, just in time, as a...portal...of some kind opened in what had been a blank wall of dirt and rock.

A glowing portal, swirling with energies not of this realm. Morgan's inner cat had the knowledge, but Morgan had never seen or even heard of anything like what she was seeing in her human existence.

And then, a man stepped through the portal.

No. Wait. Not a man...

A fey.

CHAPTER NINE

The newcomer stopped short and looked around, a puzzled expression lighting his fair-skinned face.

"Now, what do we have here?" The stranger surveyed the small chamber. "Matthew Redstone, as I live and breathe."

"Cam?" Matt asked, stepping forward in the suddenly much smaller space. "Where the hell did you come from?"

"Underhill," the one Matt had called Cam answered briefly. "This mine has been a sort of doorway to the fey realm for centuries, lad. But what's happened to the tunnel? Are ye trapped?"

"Earthquakes. Unnatural tremors caused by bloodpath mages we suspect are *Venifucus*. We were spying on them deeper in the mine when everything started shaking," Matt explained as Cam's expression grew more concerned with each word. "We ran, but we only made it this far before the tunnel collapsed around us."

"This is grave news, lad. Grave news." Cam scowled. "But who is your lassie?"

"I guess you never met the Brotherhood's lawyer the last time we worked together." Matt's expression brightened as he turned to Morgan. "Miss Morgan Chase, this is Cameron of the fey realm. He was an ally during the trouble at the time of Sebastian and Christy's mating."

Cam came closer and took Morgan's hand, bowing over it in a charmingly old-fashioned way. Morgan couldn't help but smile, even as the walls felt like they were closing in with two big men taking up all the space in their dirt and rock prison.

"Pleased to meet you. Can you help us get out of here?" She knew she sounded weak, but she couldn't help it. She'd held off the fear as long as she could and was now on her last legs of courage and resolve. Surely, a fey would be able to get them out.

Cam rose and looked deep into her eyes. His smile made her feel a little better, but his words were music to her ears.

"Of course, milady." He let go of her hand and turned to face the wall of dirt and rocks they'd been digging through.

Cam made a few gestures with his hands, and suddenly, the dirt flowed away from the rocks. Then, the rocks rolled in an orderly march downward and around, to line the sides of the tunnel, reinforcing it. Within thirty seconds, the tunnel had been cleared and strengthened by the lining of rocks along the sides to a depth of two additional feet.

Cameron continued his work, gaining another two feet every thirty seconds or so. Morgan watched his progress, amazed at such casual use of impressive magic. Although, she'd seen other people work magic over the years, she had never seen anything quite like this. The power of the fey was legendary for good reason, she was discovering.

Within a few minutes, Morgan felt fresh air flowing down the tunnel as Cam broke through to the other side. Other scents came to her nose too. A particular tang of blood hit her nose, and she recognized Marc's scent. It was full dark out now, and he had, indeed, come to help.

"Marc?" she whispered.

"Morgan?" came the answering, cautious reply.

"We're here," she said softly, joyfully.

"I'll have the tunnel completely clear in another ten seconds, Master LaTour," Cam said, his voice distinctive with a slight brogue.

"Cameron? Is that you?" Marc's voice carried down the

tunnel, his tone indicating his surprise.

"One and the same. Your friends here needed a hand, and I happened to be in the neighborhood." The fey chuckled, even as he ended the spell that had reopened and reinforced the tunnel. He stepped confidently forward, and Matt took Morgan's hand, walking with her through the newly-cleared tunnel. Sure enough, Marc was waiting on the other end.

Marc shook hands with Cameron, a bemused expression on his face. "It's good to see you again, Cameron," Marc said politely. "Strange to find you here, but good, all the same."

"Not so strange as you might think," Cameron said as he let go of the Master's hand. "Fey often use such places as entrance points into your realm. Our realm is called Underhill by mortals for a reason, after all. When the humans of old saw my brethren popping out from such places in ancient times, they thought we all lived in caves or some such. We let them think it. Chalk it up to our race's sometimes perverse sense of humor." Cameron chuckled as Matt and Morgan joined them.

Matt reached out to shake Marc's hand. "Thank you for coming to our rescue," he said politely.

"Looks like I'm a little late for the rescue part, but we did see something interesting while we were searching for you," Marc said in a quiet voice that wouldn't carry beyond their small group. "We've been spread out over this mountain since just after twilight, looking for your tracks. We've found at least two entrances to the mine that weren't on any map. The discovery of the dead snake you must have run into earlier in the day led us to watch the entrance nearest it. Atticus is still there, working that entrance, but after the last tremor and then watching as the sorcerers traipsed out of there congratulating themselves, we all decided to track from different angles."

"You saw Irma?" Morgan asked.

"In the flesh. Irma and two other men. One of whom Atticus recognized as Irma's husband, Carlos. He had a file on them, and you can be sure my old friend is kicking himself for having missed the mole in his own organization. But we can save the recriminations for later. Ian and Bernard broke off the search here to follow the mages. There's no one on the mountain but our people now."

"I should go to the entrance the sorcerers accessed," Cam said quickly, frowning. "I'd like to examine the kinds of magic they are using."

"I hoped you would say that," Marc answered, nodding at the fey. "I'm not ashamed to admit that we could use your kind of help on this, Cameron."

"I'd be honored," Cam replied. "And now that you know part of this mine is one of my favorite portals to Underhill, I suppose I need to make nice with the land owner," he added with a wink.

"Not just Atticus, but the wolves who'll be living here too, I suspect," Marc said, one eyebrow raised. "Now, are you two all right?" Marc redirected his interest to Matt and Morgan. In fact, he walked over and put his hands on Morgan's shoulders. "I know it couldn't have been easy for you."

"It wasn't," Morgan admitted, smiling up at the man who'd had such a great impact on her life. "But Matt was with me. He helped a lot." She looked over at Matt, knowing she was admitting to something here. She was telling Marc—essentially her father figure—about her new boyfriend, albeit in an oblique way.

They started walking, all four of them, toward the previously hidden entrance that Irma and her people had used. Marc shot her a few concerned looks but let the moment pass without comment on Matt's presence being so *helpful* to her. She suspected he'd quiz her later, but for now, he was apparently more concerned with the bigger picture, thank goodness.

"I'm texting the others to let them know you're safe," Marc said, already tapping out a message on his cell phone. "I'm going to set up a perimeter around the hidden mine entrance so we can be certain we remain alone up here while we investigate."

"Excellent plan." Cameron nodded. "Now, why don't you two tell us the tale from the beginning while we walk? I confess I'm very curious as to how you ended up where you did."

"We were checking out something one of the eco people told us about there being something off in the mine," Morgan explained. "The girl's name is Rosalie O'Hanlan. I sent you an email about what she told us." She nodded to Marc.

"I saw it. I've got someone doing a background check on her as we speak," Marc said. "So, you were acting on her intel and came up here to nose around a bit?"

"We thought we'd take a look," Matt agreed, picking up the narrative. "We watched the entrances we knew about, then decided to roam a bit in our fur to look for anything out of the ordinary. We found the snake—"

"What kind of snake?" Cameron asked, interrupting Matt's report.

"You can see for yourself. It's right up there." Matt nodded toward the spot on the small rise that Morgan had blundered into earlier in the day.

Cam set off more quickly than Morgan would have thought the man could move. Marc stayed with them while Cam took a quick look around.

"Nasty work, that," Marc observed, gesturing toward the snake.

Cam came back quickly, his expression grim. "Worse than you know. If I'm not much mistaken, the body is laid out in the exact pattern of the fault line beneath our feet. It reeks of evil magic."

Nobody said anything as they began walking again. Finally, Morgan decided to finish the story of their adventure, so as to get it out of the way. It was bad enough to remember it. She didn't want to have to talk about it too much. Better to forget the trauma and move on.

"We spotted the hidden entrance and decided to investigate. We were able to get pretty close. Close enough to see some of the chanting and feel that last tremor from inside. We made a run for it, but we didn't make it all the way out. The tunnel collapsed on either side of us." She shuddered but pushed on in her story. "Matt's phone was destroyed, and mine only had a little charge left. We decided to wait until dark to call, but while we were digging, the portal opened, and he stepped out." She gestured toward Cameron.

"You left out one thing, lass," Cameron surprised her by saying. For a moment, she wondered if he was referring to the way Matt and she had passed the time. Had he been spying on them while they were making love? "At some point..." he went on, "...somebody started praying."

Morgan frowned. "I did. But how could you know that?"

"Because She whom I serve sent me to you in your hour of need," he answered, astounding her. "I've operated in secret for centuries, but the Mother of All has decreed it is now time for Her chosen Knights to reveal ourselves. I'm a *Chevalier de la Lumiere*—a Knight of the Light. I serve the Goddess. She sent me through that portal to answer your prayer."

Morgan stopped in her tracks, as did the rest of them. Cameron faced them, smiling faintly. A momentary flash of another image superimposed itself on his body—it was him, but he was dressing in glowing armor, with a brightly flaming sword at his side. His knightly form, she imagined, stunned by the revelation.

"I—" she began, not really knowing what to say. "Thank you, Sir Cameron. And Blessed Be the Mother of All for answering my prayer. I never thought..."

The glowing image of Cameron as a Knight faded, and he smiled kindly at her. "She hears and sees all, Morgan. She knows your heart and chose to intervene by sending me. Much as She sent Marc to you all those years ago. You have a greater purpose than you know, and perhaps, the two of you together..." he pointed between her and Matt, "...are meant to do something important in the fight against evil. Perhaps you've already done it." He smiled again as he moved forward, starting them all walking again.

As they neared the hidden entrance to the mine, other members of the Brotherhood stepped out of the dark to join them. Atticus and Sebastian came over to them, the others dispersing to form a perimeter. It looked like Marc had sent out a call for help to most of his top people, and many had answered.

Several of the vampires nodded to Morgan before fading back into the darkness. She had worked with most of the Brotherhood at one point or another on their many legal dealings and counted many of them as friends. She was pleased to see that so many had come to help.

"Glad to see you in one piece," Sebastian said, clapping Matt on the back as he joined them.

Atticus was a bit more reserved. "Are you all right, Morgan?" he asked, concern in his expression.

"I'm fine. Cameron came to our rescue," she said, uncomfortable being the center of attention.

Both Atticus and Sebastian greeted Cameron, renewing their acquaintance. Morgan stood quietly, feeling a bit apprehensive about whether they'd ask her to go back into the mine. She shifted from foot to foot, nervous.

Matt took her hand discreetly, squeezing it in reassurance. Just like that, her nerves settled. All it took was his touch to ground her and remind her that she wasn't alone. Matt was with her. And with him at her side, she could do anything.

They spent the next hours retracing their steps into the mine, explaining what they'd seen and heard while the others examined everything in minute detail. Cameron observed all and offered insight into what the magic users had been doing. They came back out of the mine, eventually, much to Morgan's relief, to find Ian guarding the entrance.

She remembered that Marc had sent Ian off to follow Irma and her cronies. If he was back, he'd have something to report. She wondered what he'd learned.

Marc greeted his enforcer—which was the vital role Ian played in the Brotherhood—and asked him to give his report. Morgan was glad Marc was sharing the information so freely.

After what she'd been through that day, she didn't want to be kept out of the loop on anything pertaining to Irma and her ilk.

"I trailed Irma and Carlos to their home, then did what I could to listen in. They've got many layers of magical protections around their dwelling, but I was able to eavesdrop on a bit of their conversation. They were very pleased with themselves," Ian reported. "And very drained by what they did tonight. They discussed giving the fault a few days to *perk*—as they put it—while they recovered their strength for another round."

"Did they say why they were doing this?" Morgan asked.

"It is as we feared. They spoke of breaching the veil between worlds in order to bring their *Mater Priori* back from the farthest realms," Ian intoned. Everyone stilled.

"Blasted Elspeth!" Cam cursed. "That bedamned woman causes chaos, even when she's not here."

"So, they definitely are *Venifucus*," Matt observed.

"There is little doubt of it," Ian confirmed. Silence followed his words, for a long moment.

Finally, Atticus broke the tension. "Well, then. I propose we leave this place, for now. Cameron, Morgan and Matt, I invite you back to my home for what's left of the night, since it is closest. Marc?" He looked expectantly at the Master, who was also one of his oldest and dearest friends, Morgan knew.

"I left Kelly there with Lissa," Marc said casually, looking tired, for once. Weariness was something Morgan wasn't used to seeing from the Master vampire who had guided so much of her life. "Perhaps, we can use some of that computer equipment you keep bragging about to further our research."

Atticus smiled. "Most definitely," he agreed, already turning with Marc to walk away.

The vampires, Morgan knew, had other means of travel. Most of the Brotherhood could shift into dark raptors or owls. Some were even powerful enough to travel as mist or smoke. But she and Matt would have to hoof it back to their vehicle. She wasn't sure about Cameron.

"Can we offer you a ride?" she asked politely, turning to the fey.

Cam nodded. "I would appreciate it. Traveling magically in this realm is too obvious to do it casually."

"Obvious in what way?" she asked as they started walking down through the woods.

"Magically," Cam explained. "If anyone is watching for fey magic—and I have to believe the *Venifucus* are watching for anything out of the ordinary—then they could find me pretty easily by following my energy trail. Best to avoid using anything too showy unless absolutely necessary."

"But what about when you showed up in the mine? Won't they be able to trace you from that?" Morgan asked as they neared the spot where they'd parked.

"Moving through an established gate from Underhill to this realm doesn't usually give off any telltale magic," Cam said, his words slower as he seemed to think. "I believe the reason that section of the tunnel didn't collapse on you was because our gate was there. They were constructed eons ago, and their presence hidden with magic the likes of which doesn't really exist anymore." Cam's tone grew even more pensive. "You two were very lucky—or perhaps, I should say *blessed*—to have been in the exact right spot when the tunnel came down around you. If you'd been a few yards either way, the outcome would have been...well...bad."

"We would've died," Morgan realized, whispering.

Matt walked up beside her, his arm coming around her shoulders. "But we didn't. We're okay, and we're going to put a stop to the bastards that caused all this trouble. Right?" He squeezed her shoulders and leaned down to kiss her temple.

She drew strength from his touch, his presence, his bold words. She couldn't be afraid—not while Matt held her. He was all that was good in this world.

"Right," she agreed, leaning up to place a kiss on his lips that wanted to be so much more. But Cam was waiting and so were the bloodletters. They had places to go and plans to make.

CHAPTER TEN

Atticus welcomed them, a few minutes later, after they'd parked in his drive. Everyone was already gathered in the home theatre that was doubling as a war room, of sorts. Atticus led them first to a guest suite, though, so they could tidy up a bit after their ordeal in the dusty tunnel. After a quick shower and change of clothes, thoughtfully supplied by Lissa, they joined the meeting already in progress in the home theatre room.

The easy chairs had been moved to the sides of the room and a big table set in the center with rolling office chairs on one side, facing the big theatre screen. Computer equipment was set up all over the table, and it looked like Atticus was in the process of placing a video call.

Cam saw Matt and Morgan at the door and signaled them over. He had two more of the rolling office chairs ready for them.

"You're just in time," Cam said with a hint of a smile as they took their seats. "Marc is calling your people."

"Grif?" Matt asked, frowning. He hadn't had a chance to call home yet and tell Grif about the problems they'd encountered.

"No…" Cam trailed off as the big screen at the front of the room came to life. It wasn't Grif, or any of Matt's other brothers. No, the Master vampire had called the Lords.

"Sorry to call so late," Marc began as the twin werewolves who were the leaders of all *were* in North America came into view.

"No problem," answered the twin on the left. "What's going on?"

"One of yours discovered something you need to know about. Apparently, it's not only volcanoes we need to watch. We just learned that the *Venifucus* here are trying to set off the San Andreas."

The twin on the right cursed while the one on the left frowned. "You're kidding, right?" asked the frowning twin.

"Sadly, no. Two of my *were* friends were caught up in a tunnel collapse after witnessing the sorcerers at work. They got help from another friend—I believe you know Cameron—to get out." The twin on the right nodded toward Cam, acknowledging him while Marc gestured to Matt and Morgan. "This is my ward, Morgan Chase, and I'm not sure if you've met Matt Redstone."

Matt stood in respect for the twin Alphas who ruled all *were* on this continent.

"We didn't hear anything from your brother on this," the twin on the left said with a trace of displeasure in his voice.

"That's because he doesn't know. I haven't had a chance to call him yet," Matt defended his Clan leader.

"We only just arrived back from the mine on my property where this happened," Atticus put in with a placating smile. "Give the boy a chance."

Matt bristled at being called a boy, but to an ancient like Atticus, Matt knew he probably seemed very young. It was something you had to get used to if you were going to hang around with bloodletters.

"This is the mine where you're building that experimental shifter housing, right?" one of the twins asked.

Matt couldn't tell the twins apart, except that one seemed to be a little more hotheaded than the other. Matt was impressed that the Lords seemed to know all about Atticus's pet project—building housing for his new werewolf employees. Maybe the Lords really were as hand-on as Grif had claimed.

"The very same," Atticus answered. "Turns out, a woman who's been working in the winery office is some kind of *Venifucus* mole." His expression tightened. "That's on me. I vet my employees carefully, and I have no idea how she slipped through, but you can be damn sure it won't happen again."

"It won't, but don't be so hard on yourself," Cam interjected, drawing everyone's attention and several surprised looks. "I will verify what was done, if it settles your mind, but you'd better believe a mage with the level of skill and power to wake a seismic fault in the earth would think nothing of sneaking past your guard. The sad truth is, as good as your security and background checks are, some magics—especially those originating in other realms—are just not going to be visible to you."

"Like the portal to Underhill?" Morgan asked shrewdly, earning a respectful nod from Cam.

"Exactly so, milady," Cam agreed. "The *Venifucus* started with Elspeth and, much as I hate to admit it, she is fey. She taught her followers certain things from other realms that should never have been known to this place and time." Cam let that sink in before continuing. "The traitor passed what I'm sure was a very thorough examination by yourself and your people, Atticus, through no fault of your own. You simply didn't know what to look for. And even if you had, it takes a very special kind of magical sensitivity to actually detect it."

"I take it you can detect such things?" Marc asked Cam pointedly. The fey warrior nodded, his head tilted to the side in respect. "Then, I hope you will stick around for a while and help us stop the chain of events these mages hope to set in motion." It was a question posed as a statement, and again, Cam nodded his assent. "I propose we wake the Redstone Alpha and get him in on this call, so Matt and Morgan will only have to recount their tale once."

As soon as the Lords agreed, Atticus dialed Grif, speaking to him privately, for a moment, before adding him to the middle-of-the-night conference call. When he showed on the screen, Grif's hair was sticking up on one side. He had big time bed head, but Matt wasn't even tempted to tease his oldest brother about it. Things were way too serious, right now, though he was glad to see the reassuring face of his big brother.

"Sorry for the lateness of the call, Alpha," Marc began, addressing Grif. "As you can see, we're on conference with your Lords. There have been troubling developments here concerning the *Venifucus*, your Clan members and your brother. Matt and Morgan are about to brief us on events from their point of view."

Marc gestured to Matt, and he knew it was show time. He and Morgan jointly explained the events that had led up to them being trapped in the collapsed mine tunnel. At that point, Cam put in his two cents, and they finished the summary of events that had led them to this point. Marc took over the meeting again, talking through the possibilities and what they planned to do next.

By the time the meeting drew to an end, little was left of the night, and the vampires started making moves toward their homes. They would have to be out of the action for the day, but left the *weres* plenty to do while they slept, away from the sun. The Lords had pledged full cooperation from both themselves and any who answered to them.

Likewise, Grif had promised the full support of all Redstone Clan personnel in the area and offered to send more to help. Marc accepted both pledges of help with grave sincerity, promising his Brotherhood's full cooperation, as well. Atticus had agreed to house and support the additional Clan members Grif was sending to assist. They could easily be hidden among the existing work crews, and Atticus seemed only too glad to have more *weres* prowling his lands by day while he and his mate slept.

The first of the additional troops would start arriving from Las Vegas later that day. But Matt and Morgan had been up going on twenty-plus hours and needed to rest for a bit before they tackled what came next. Atticus offered them a guest suite in his house, and they accepted gladly. Cameron, too, would be housed in Atticus's mansion above ground while Atticus and Lissa slept in their hidden home below.

The guest suite had two bedrooms and a shared sitting room and bath. Morgan didn't hesitate to join Matt in his chosen bedroom the moment she was out of the shower. Things had changed between them in that mine. Shared danger and the threat of death had cemented the bond she had been worried about before. Now, there was little doubt left in her mind. Matt Redstone was as good as they come. As good as gold.

She chuckled inwardly. It had taken getting buried alive in an abandoned gold mine to make her realize that life was too precious to waste it being scared of every little thing. Being scared of losing her identity to love had been her greatest problem, but no more.

Oh, sure, she still had a bit of anxiety over how everything was going to work out with Matt's family. *He* was a good guy, but she hadn't met all his brothers or their mates, yet. His family might be a nightmare like hers had been. She'd have to wait and see on that.

But her doubts about Matt had gone, and she was ready to embrace life. And love. And him.

Not necessarily in that order, she thought with another inward smile as she slid her arms around his waist. Matt turned in her arms, and she realized he must've taken a quick shower somewhere else because his hair was wet and dust-free for the first time since the cave in at the mine. Usually golden blonde and slightly curly, it was dark, now, sitting close against the contours of his head. And he looked good enough to eat.

He smelled clean too. The bloodletters had sensitive noses

and stocked their houses with scentless soaps and herbal products that sat well with shifter sensibilities. Morgan had found a shampoo with a lovely balsam scent that reminded her of the outdoors, and Matt scented of fresh herbs that made her want to lick him all over.

Or...maybe that wasn't the only thing that made her want to do that. He was, after all, an Alpha of her species, with an Alpha's traits and build. He was lean but muscular in all the right ways. Handsome as all get out and sensitive to her feelings—as he'd proven, time and again, especially when she'd been freaking out in that dark, cramped, dusty mine.

She knew many shifters—especially the wolves—liked such places to raise their young, but Morgan would be just as glad if she never had to set foot in that mine again. It made her shiver just to think about it. No, siree. No way was she going down there for anything less than the fate of the world being in her hands.

Then again...it sort of was. Or it had been earlier that day.

"What makes you frown like that, sweetheart?" Matt's voice was gentle as he drew back to look into her eyes. His fingertips grazed her cheek, his gaze narrowing in concern.

She turned her face into his open palm. "You were magnificent in the mine. You never lost your cool. You were so good to me..." She kissed his palm. "You're one hell of an Alpha, Matt. You might be the youngest of the infamous Redstone Five, but you're definitely the best of them." She reached upward to place a light kiss on his lips. "I'm glad you're mine," she whispered.

She felt his whole body tense. "You really mean that?"

He seemed to be holding his breath, waiting for her reply. She laid her cheek against his shoulder, her hand over his racing heart.

"You're my mate," she answered simply.

"Sweet Mother of All, that sounds good." His breath left him in a rush, as did his tension. His arms tightened around her, squeezing in joy as she felt the relief in his every muscle. "I thought there might be something between us when we first met, but you were so tough on me, Miss Morgan, I barely escaped with my hide intact from your icy lawyer glare."

He was laughing as he said it, and she realized she'd been very stand-offish when they first met. She hadn't wanted to be around shifters, but Marc had forced her hand. Her anger at being outed to a cougar Alpha was really more aimed at Marc, but Matt had suffered the brunt of her displeasure in that brief meeting.

"Yeah, I was kind of a bitch, wasn't I?" she agreed, laughing along with him. "Sorry. I wasn't really angry with you, but with the whole situation. I was very happy living among the Brotherhood with no shifter friends, and then, Marc landed me in it with you. I was so afraid you were going to force me back into the fold, or whatever devious thing I had in my mind about shifters, back then. I'm sorry. I was very wrong about you."

"Water under the bridge," Matt said graciously. "And you had good reason for your suspicions about our kind. It'll be my honor and privilege to show you what shifter life is really like... If you'll let me."

He seemed hesitant, and she knew she'd given him cause to wonder about her commitment to the mating. She had some work to do to clear that up in his mind. She didn't ever want him to be uncertain of her again.

"Let you? Matt, I don't know about where you come from, but even in my screwed up Clan, mating was for life." She smiled up at him, glad to see the relief and joy in his eyes. "Like it or not, you're stuck with me now. And I give you fair warning—I have a life and career here. The Brotherhood needs me more often than not. I'm not comfortable around shifters—though I'm willing to try, for your sake. But, if things get too much to handle, you can always find me here."

"Find you?" He squeezed her tight and carried her to the bed. "Honey, I'm never letting you go. If my family scares you, screw 'em. You're all I need to be happy for the rest of my life." He showered her with kisses as he untied the belt of her terrycloth robe. "My home is with you, wherever we end up."

"Then, you don't mind if I continue working?" she asked, needing to know, even if her blood was beginning to overheat from his nearness.

"Mind? Morgan…" He paused, resting on his elbows so he could look into her eyes. "I never, in my wildest dreams, thought my mate would be a high-powered attorney, but I couldn't be prouder of you, or more willing to let you be who you are. If you want to practice law, I'm certain the Clan— and the Brotherhood—would have a place for you. For the record, I never wanted my mate to be the *little woman*, barefoot and pregnant and all that. I want a partner. Someone to stand by my side, not behind me. In short, counselor, I want you."

He dipped his head and captured her lips in one of the most romantic moments of her life. Matt Redstone was like no other man. He was everything she hadn't known she wanted in a mate. He was perfect for her in pretty much every way that counted. Almost too good to be true, but then, that's what mating was supposed to be all about, right? A little divine intervention to pair up shifters with their perfect matches.

Morgan hadn't believed it before, but after meeting Matt, she was definitely a true believer now. She kissed him back with all her might and moaned when he broke away from her lips to trail his mouth over her bare skin, down over her collarbones, onto her chest, and then, his tongue darted out to tease her nipples—first one, then the other—as his big hands shaped her softness to his liking.

His fingers had calluses that added a delicious friction to his touch on her overheated skin. Everywhere his fingers trailed, fire followed in their wake. The fire of passion, of desire, of…love.

She wanted him inside her, and she wanted it now. The foreplay was nice, but after the past hours, she needed the touch of her mate almost desperately.

She felt the edge of the mattress touch the backs of her legs, and relief flooded through her overheating body. Matt continued to kiss her and suck on delicate, needy bits of her skin, but she wanted more. She wanted all of him. Now.

She squealed happily when Matt lifted her by the waist and dropped her playfully to the exact center of the mattress below. She bounced only once before Matt's hard body stopped all motion by coming down over her, covering her with his muscular warmth. She looked deep into his eyes and saw the flashing topaz there that echoed the need in her own soul. The need for him. For her mate.

"Don't keep me waiting," she pled her case, her voice unsteady. "I need you now."

His eyes flared, and she knew he felt the same deep need. Her robe was gone, and he was naked, too. She'd lost track of how that had happened, but it didn't matter. All that really mattered was Matt. Here. In her arms. In her body. She couldn't wait any longer.

Morgan wrapped her legs around his, pulling him to her. They were face to face, and she held his wild gaze as she drew him closer. He accommodated her desires, following her lead. He hesitated only momentarily to find just the right spot before sliding hard inside her.

Heaven.

He filled her completely, the perfect match for her in every way.

And then, he began to move. She hadn't thought it could feel any better, but each time they joined their bodies, Matt took her to new levels of passion. She began to come almost immediately and just kept on coming. Her body shook as he plunged into her, time and again, speaking of his love, his joy in mating her, his need and his claiming. She rode the waves of ever-increasing rapture, following where he led her into realms she hadn't even dreamed existed.

At the very last, he dropped his mouth to her neck and bit her.

She screamed as the greatest climax she'd ever experienced

claimed her. The pain in the curve of her neck was as nothing. It only added to the stark agony of pleasure that made every muscle in her body tense and cry out in joy.

Morgan hadn't known anything could feel so good, or last so long. Matt kept her at the height of her climax for long minutes during which she touched the stars and fell back to earth in his arms. Matt held her throughout, his tongue laving the place where he'd bit her. His teeth had almost reverted to their normal human shape by the time she was aware enough to realize they had transformed partially to deliver a half-shifted bite mark. Human-sized but from pointed, predator teeth.

She hadn't even known that could happen during sex, but what a way to find out! She wanted it again. Maybe not right this very moment, but she knew the bite of her mate had excited her inner cat as much as it had her human side. There was something primal, and incredibly sexy, about being claimed by the beast, as well as the man.

She could finally share every facet of who she was as a person, and as a shifter, with her lover—her mate. She had never been able to do that before, and she felt a freedom in her heart that made her spirit light. She was free to be herself with Matt, which was something new and precious.

"I love you, Matt Redstone," she whispered, her heart overflowing.

He tugged her closer, his arm still around her, though he'd shifted to her side so he wouldn't crush her with his weight. His calloused fingers rubbed little circles over her abdomen.

"And I love you, Morgan Chase. You're my mate, but will you also be my bride?" He leaned up on one elbow to look at her hopefully.

Among shifters, mating was as good as—actually better than—human marriage. Her Clan hadn't bothered with the human ceremony, but she knew the Brotherhood often legalized their matings in the human legal system, as well as by their own traditions. Maybe Matt's Clan did the same?

"You want to marry me?" she asked, to be sure.

"With all my heart. Our souls already know we're mates, but I want everyone to know—human and Other alike—that we belong to each other. I want to celebrate our mating with my Clan, but also with your human friends and business associates. I want everyone to know that you're mine." She felt her stomach clench at the glint in his eye. She liked his possessive side, though it frightened her a bit too. He must've seen that tiny bit of apprehension, because he tempered his words by adding, "And I'm yours."

He dipped his head to kiss her then. It was a gentle kiss filled with love that left her in no doubt that his possessiveness wasn't anything to fear, but rather to embrace...because her inner cat was just as fiercely possessive of him as he was of her. They were a match, and her cat wanted everyone to know it.

CHAPTER ELEVEN

"We were going to meet at the winery office, but Irma's been working there for months. There's no way to be sure she hasn't set up some sort of magical surveillance on the place. Cameron will go over every inch of the grounds later, but for now, the safest place to meet up with the Clan werewolves is on their territory," Matt told her.

Morgan wasn't all that eager to go into a werewolf den. First off, she was a cat, and her inner cat didn't like being surrounded by a wolf Pack. This was on top of the fact that, until very recently, Morgan hadn't been exactly *comfortable* around shifters. But she took heart from the fact that her mate would be at her side. Matt knew these people, and she trusted his judgment.

So it was that Morgan found herself seated at a huge table in the giant house the werewolves were using as what Matt had called a *Pack house* while waiting for their permanent homes to be completed. Jenny sat at the head of the table with Philomena sharing the place of honor. The two Alpha females seemed to be good friends, if Morgan was any judge of their body language.

They'd left room for Matt and Morgan at the other end of the table, their families filling in the spaces all around. Drinks had already been served—soda mostly, with the occasional beer thrown in. Matt and Morgan were offered their choice of beverage and both accepted steaming mugs of coffee with thanks to the younger members of the wolf Pack, who served them.

This was really Morgan's first look at a wolf Pack in their own environment, so to speak. Up until now, she'd watched the werewolf women from a distance, preferring to keep herself separate from the shifters who had come to work for Atticus. Morgan realized that had been a mistake.

There were a majority of women around this giant table, but there were also men scattered through the crowd. Philomena's sons and the husbands of some of the other crew members. From what Morgan observed, nobody was subservient in a bad way to anyone else, though they all respected the Alphas among them.

And there were different degrees of Alpha-ness, for lack of a different word. The minute Matt came in, they'd all immediately deferred to him in a way they hadn't to the others. Morgan sensed that she, too, was being afforded some deference, though she had no idea what she'd done to earn it. The younger members of the wolf Pack were speaking to her with the same kind of friendly, but respectful tone they used to address Jenny or Philomena.

Interesting.

"Thanks for meeting with us here," Matt said, which seemed to call the meeting to order. Everyone quieted down and sat attentively, watching him. "There have been some developments, and it's become clear that there's a mole in the winery office. What do you all know of Irma?"

"She smells funny," one youngster piped up. Even the cubs were at this meeting, which surprised Morgan, and the child who'd spoken wasn't chastised. It seemed all were given a chance to speak at this sort of meeting.

Matt looked at the little boy, sitting on his mama's lap. "What does she smell like to you, JayJay?" he asked gently.

"Bad," the boy answered shyly, reaching for his mother's hand. "She tried to give me a lolly, but I didn't want it from her, and then, she looked mean at me when Mama wasn't watching."

The boy couldn't be more than five years old. Probably younger, though Morgan wasn't such a good judge of such things, having spent precious little time around children. But this boy had sensed something about Irma that the adults—and the Brotherhood's best investigators—had missed.

"You've got very sharp senses, JayJay. You're right to trust them," Matt praised the boy, and it was clear the child was pleased with Matt's public display of approval. He beamed while his mother hugged him close. "Did anybody else notice anything funny about her?" Matt asked again.

Heads shook all around, along with confused expressions. Some eyes held worry—and rightly so, Morgan realized.

"Don't feel bad if you didn't notice what JayJay did," Matt said, offering some comfort to the others. "It turns out Irma is a *Venifucus* mage. Morgan and I saw her with our own eyes, working some kind of dark magic to stir the fault deep in the mine. She and two males—one of whom is her husband, Carlos. We're still working on identifying the second male. From here on out, I want you all to stay as far away from Irma as possible. And if you see her anywhere near here, call me immediately. Or if one of the Brotherhood is nearby, tell them. We're formulating a plan to stop Irma and her comrades, but we haven't finalized it yet."

Questions flew at that point, and Matt and Morgan both recounted what had happened to them in the mine. Most of the Pack already knew the bare bones of the story, but none had heard all the gory details yet. They'd just gotten to the part where Cameron showed up when the doorbell rang.

Jenny went to answer it and came back with the man himself. Matt made the introductions as room was made for Cam at the big table. Since he wasn't a shifter, they didn't seem to know where to place him, at first, but Matt solved the problem by moving his chair back and over a bit so Cam could sit next to him, in a spare chair brought by one of the younger wolves.

Matt watched the reactions of the wolf Pack carefully. Most of the predominantly female gathering seemed suspicious and unsure of Cam, but when Matt looked at little JayJay, it was clear adoration he saw in the child's eyes when he looked at Cam. It seemed little JayJay had a level of perception about magic the rest of his family didn't appear to have. That would bear further watching in the years to come, and Matt made a mental note to mention it to Grif, as Clan Alpha, and to the boy's mother.

"Thank you, lass," Cam said, smiling kindly at the young girl who brought him coffee. "And thank you all for welcoming me into your midst," he said to the wider group. His brogue was in full effect, and the women watched him skeptically but with a willingness to hear him out that boded well for this meeting.

"What are you, Mister Cam?" JayJay asked out of turn, causing his mother to try to hush him, but Cameron only smiled at the boy.

"I'm fey," Cameron answered into the silence of the room. All eyes were watching him.

"But you're more, Mister Cam," JayJay insisted.

Cam tilted his head. "Aye, laddie, I'm a fey knight, and I serve the Mother of All and her Light," he announced simply. "It seems our Lady gave you a little more perception than the rest of your Clan. Keep your senses sharp and tell your elders when you see something that doesn't seem right to you. It is your duty to help protect the Pack."

Cameron spoke to the little boy with all seriousness, and Jay responded to the tone, nodding gravely. "I will, Mister Cam." He turned to his mother, looking up at her. "I'm sorry I didn't say about Miss Irma before."

His mother kissed him and hugged him tight.

"That's okay, little man," Matt stepped in, talking in a low voice to Jay. "You didn't know how important it was before. Now, you do. And, now, we know you are an excellent watcher, JayJay. We'll need your talents in the days to come."

"You can count on me, Alpha," Jay was quick to proclaim.

"There is the little matter of safe passage," Cam said into the silence, as the conversation turned. "The gold mine has long been a place where some of us cross from Underhill into this realm. The gateway is sealed from the rest of the mine now by a cave-in, but since you will be using parts of the mine as your den, I would not want to trespass in any way. I recognize the mine as yours, but I would request that I be granted safe passage from the gateway to the surface and through your lands to the outside world."

"Is the gateway dangerous?" Jenny asked.

Cam regarded her, tilting his head as he considered his answer. "To those with no magic, it doesn't really exist," he said at last, but then, expounded. "But some of your Clan have magic and to them, it could be a bit of a problem. If they triggered it, they would end up in the fey realm and find it difficult to get back without assistance. I would, of course, help anyone so afflicted in any way I could, but time doesn't pass the same way between our two realms, and that could cause problems for any unwitting travelers. It would be best if that particular access tunnel was made off limits to all but fey who might be traveling between realms."

"Who else, besides yourself, might be using the gateway?" Philomena asked next.

"This gateway is only known to those of my Order," Cam answered cooly.

Philomena surprised Matt with her wide-eyed reaction. "Are you a *Chevalier*, Sir?"

"What do you know of us?" Cam asked, not upset by her question, but rather seeming to be intrigued.

"When I was very young, I nearly fell to my death while I was exploring on a mountainside," she said, surprising Matt. Judging by the expressions of those gathered, nobody had known of this particular event from her past. "I ended up falling off a cliff and landing on a ledge that was barely wide enough for my shifted form. My leg was broken, and I had no way to climb up the rock face either in wolf or human form. I prayed to the Lady, and two days later, I was rescued by a *Chevalier de la Lumiere*. He got me off that ledge and healed my leg. He was amazing, and so kind. He also told me that, one day, I would meet another like him, and the whole world would be in jeopardy."

"I'm sorry, lass," Cam said softly. "This is that day, and my brother was correct. The *Venifucus* threat is real, and we of the Light are coming back into this realm in larger numbers, working with those here who are on the side of the Light to defeat the darkness."

Silence reigned for a moment while everyone took in the seriousness of his words.

"Cameron is known to the Clan," Matt said firmly when Jenny looked at him. "He is what he claims, and he has helped us in the past. Grif has authorized every member of the Clan to aid him in his mission in any way we can."

"Then, safe passage is the least we can do," Jenny said after only a moment's hesitation. "With the proviso that the gate and the tunnel leading to the surface are made no-go zones for our young and ourselves, unless under dire threat. I'd also like to know if there's a way we can contact you if you're Underhill. Is there some way we can get messages to you, Sir Cameron, if we have news to share or need your help?"

Cam looked impressed. "Aye. I can put up wardings that will let me know if one of yours says the proper words near the gateway. Will that do?"

Jenny smiled. "I think we have an accord."

* * *

Matt and Morgan stayed at the Pack house longer than she expected. The women were friendly, and Morgan was glad to get to know them. If they were any indication of the rest of the Redstone Clan, then Morgan realized she had been worried about nothing. These women were bright, intelligent and clearly respected and well-treated by everyone else in the

Clan.

When Jenny insisted they stay for dinner, Morgan couldn't refuse. The food was delicious and plentiful. So often, Morgan had to hide her shifter appetite among humans. It was kind of startling to eat with the wolf Pack and see that they ate just as much as she did, and nobody raised any eyebrows at the mass consumption of rare steak. For once in her life, Morgan didn't have to watch what she ate for fear of giving herself away.

She enjoyed every bite of her steak, munched on a turkey leg and didn't skimp on dessert either. Matt ate even more than she did and kept refilling her glass and offering her side dishes. He was attentive without being annoying. In fact, he was the perfect dinner partner, and she found herself wanting to take care of him like he was doing for her.

After a while, she became aware of some rather pointed looks from some of the older ladies. They realized something was between Morgan and Matt, but they seemed to approve, if their smiles were anything to go by. They were grinning and pushing platters toward them, watching the way Matt would serve Morgan first with nods and grins.

They talked a bit more about plans for stopping the *Venifucus* and what was going on in the mine. Some of the most vulnerable were being sent back to Las Vegas until things settled down, but Morgan was impressed by the way Matt allowed the wolf Pack to make their own decisions on who would stay and who would go. Morgan was also impressed by how many of them chose to stay and fight and how easily Matt accepted that the females would stand alongside the men in this time of crisis.

The Redstones ran their Clan quite a bit differently than her original Clan. In fact, the Redstone Clan was a far cry from what she had grown up with. All for the better. So far, she hadn't seen anything to concern her that she might be walking into a nightmare like that of her youth. No, the Redstones were what a Clan should be, and she felt truly blessed to be welcome among them.

As darkness fell, Matt and Morgan returned to Atticus's home. They went straight to the make-shift war room for an update. Irma and her husband had been under surveillance all day by *weres* and would be watched by vamps at night. Much to Morgan's relief, Irma and husband hadn't done much at all that day. By all accounts, they had slept most of the day away, appearing groggy around mid-afternoon. They'd eaten, washed up, and then had gone promptly back to bed.

Apparently, waking the San Andreas fault was exhausting work.

Cameron had traveled with them, hitching a ride once again in Matt's vehicle. He was welcomed by Atticus as host, then given a seat next to Marc, the Master vampire. Morgan and Matt sat farther down the table but were still central to the discussion. Morgan was surprised, at first, that everyone just assumed she'd sit with Matt rather than near Marc, who was both her employer and had been her protector for so many years.

A subtle shift was going on. The Brotherhood was quietly acknowledging her new relationship with Matt in a way that was both alarming and very, very comforting. It was as if she'd brought home her boyfriend to meet her family, and they approved.

She supposed, if she had been brought up in a normal Clan of shifters, she might've experienced this sort of quiet welcome when she introduced Matt. It was touching to know that the people she held dearest in the world—Marc and several other members of the Brotherhood—liked Matt and approved of her relationship with him.

It was a big change for her to be part of a couple. She felt almost as if she'd lost something. There was now a subtle emotional—and obvious physical—distance between her and Marc. Before, she would've been sitting very close, probably slightly behind him, in the role of legal advisor. Now, she was farther down the table, seated next to her mate.

She looked over at Matt, watching him as he talked with Atticus. He was her mate. That was something she could never regret, though she wasn't sure she could keep up with all the emotional changes finding him had wrought on her life. The new distance from Marc was stark and somewhat unsettling, but as if Matt realized her emotional state, he reached for her hand. He glanced her way and smiled, even as he continued to speak with Atticus. Matt held her hand, squeezing gently, offering silent comfort, and her whole world warmed with his simple, thoughtful gesture.

He was her *mate*. For better or worse, she would have to come to terms with all that meant to her life and her career. Things were different now, and there was no going back. Not that she'd want to. She would never give him up. Not for anything.

"Can we count on any further help from the fey realm?" Marc asked Cameron, drawing everyone's attention as the meeting came to order.

"While there is interest in what transpires in this realm, if only for the sake of the half-fey progeny of many of our people, the fey are rather an insular race, these days. In centuries past, we spent a lot more time in the mortal realm, but with the advancement of your technology, we have retreated more and more to our own places. There are still many half-fey, half-human children, though, and many of them have a vested interest in what goes on here. Most of them are sworn to fight Elspeth already. A few of our greatest warriors are also pledged to end Elspeth should she escape the bonds of the farthest realm, which is her prison. If that happens, the fey response will be much greater." Cameron sat back and sighed. "Unfortunately, not many believe that her followers could possibly succeed in freeing her. I'm afraid she will have to be on a rampage before the fey will come fight her in greater numbers—and the devastation of the battle will happen here, once again, as it did of old. Many innocents will die."

"Then, we are on our own to prevent it," Marc stated flatly.

Cameron sat forward once more. "Not entirely alone, my

friend. The Knights are on your side. We are not many, but we are faithful and strong. We will come to your aid and do what we can to prevent a catastrophe. But do not discount the power you yourselves wield. The Brotherhood is strong. The *were* are cunning. Together, you have already stopped many attempts to free Elspeth. Lady willing, you will continue to block the *Venifucus's* attempts to do their evil deeds."

"The way I see it, we are not organized enough," Atticus offered. "Even with our new level of cooperation with the Lords, we are only regional organizations, at best. We're not global. From all evidence, the *Venifucus* are a truly global organization. There are too many variables around the world for us to cover every possibility. We have to rely on local groups—the Lords and Masters of each different region—to coordinate the defense. Unfortunately, some of them are not what I would call on top of things."

"I would have to agree," Marc concurred. "I've also reached out to certain human magic users I've heard of who are purported to be on the side of Light. I'm sorry to say, my overtures have not been well received."

"Now, that's where I might be able to help a bit," Cam spoke up again. "I have connections with certain mages that might be useful. Humans might still fear bloodletters, but the interaction between human and fey goes back millennia. We taught them about magic to begin with, and most of the magic in your world today came originally from the fey realm. I can work with my contacts among those I know to be serving the Lady and the Light, to see what help we can gain from them."

"And the *were* have always had a good relationship with a worldwide network of Priestesses who will help in any way they can, I'm sure," Matt offered. "Several of them have already been in direct action against the *Venifucus* and are working with us."

Marc seemed to consider. "I'd almost forgotten about those estimable ladies. We should probably ask a representative from their order to join our planning sessions, in future. For right now though, we have to decide how to stop Irma and Company in their tracks."

The meeting went on as a plan was formulated. They had a little breathing room while Irma and her fellows recovered from the work they had done the day before, but it was agreed that they shouldn't wait too long. No sense in letting the sorcerers get back up to full strength before the confrontation. They had to move soon.

They didn't want to confront them in or near the mine. Not with the fault being active. The risk of energy overflow was too great, Cam cautioned. Best to fight it out as far away from the mine, as possible. Which meant they would have to confront the sorcerers in town. Preferably in their homes—which was both a problem and a solution to keeping innocent bystanders out of the fray.

The problem came in, Cam explained, in that any mage worth his salt would weave protections around his home. The good guys would have to overcome the magical protections before they could confront the bad guys, and by that time, they would almost certainly have lost the element of surprise.

But, in the case of Irma, at least, there was an alternative location that would serve. The winery office was an area Atticus could control. Cam agreed to check it for magical interference and lay down a few wardings of his own. With any luck, he'd be able to trap Irma in a web of magic before she even realized things had changed drastically at the Maxwell Winery office.

Because it was his home territory, it was natural that Atticus wanted to be the one to confront Irma. The Brotherhood decided to do that part of the job, leaving the *weres* to go after the two men. But each take-down team would have members of both races. The team going after Irma consisted of the leadership of the Brotherhood—Atticus and Marc, primarily—with Jenny's family as backup, since it wasn't out of the question to see winery workers at the office.

Morgan and Matt would go after Irma's husband with

Cam and the vampire enforcer, Ian, as backup. Philomena's work crew was going to take down the third mage, along with another of Marc's enforcers. A quick call to the Priestess Hilda confirmed that she would also be part of that group, since the two groups that were confronting the men would likely need magical assistance just to get through the wardings. Cam would do it for Matt and Morgan, but Philomena would need Hilda's help if they were all going to strike at the same time.

Monday evening—tomorrow night—at sunset, was the moment they would all strike. Irma would be working on Monday, and Atticus would send a request through that she stay late—something he often did. The work hours of those at the winery office were flexible since Atticus often scheduled dinner meetings. Everyone knew going in that they would start work later and finish later as a result. The few office workers liked the hours, since they didn't have to be in until noon, and the free gourmet dinners Atticus provided were considered a perk.

Morgan felt her inner cat perk up and pace inside her mind. She wanted to claw the evil ones for what they had done, and it began to feel like the moment for action was at hand. A certain excitement filled the room as they planned each action down to the last second. Morgan paid close attention to her part in the plan, thrilled that nobody was trying to get her to stay out of it. She owed those sorcerers for trapping her in that mine, and she was damned well going to get some payback.

CHAPTER TWELVE

"We're beginning to live like vampires," Matt observed as they entered the guest room after the meeting broke up near dawn. "I always enjoyed prowling at night, but I do need some sleep in order to function during the day."

"Welcome to my world." Morgan chuckled as she kicked off her shoes and stretched. The meeting had been long, but important. She felt good about what they'd decided and the plans they'd made for the next evening. "Since I work mostly with vampires, I tend to keep their hours. There are some days I don't ever see the sun."

Matt came over and wrapped his arms around her waist. "It's nice to have the option, though," he said philosophically, surprising her. "I can't imagine what it must be like to give up the sun completely. To not have a choice about it." He shuddered a bit, shaking his shoulders. "I like the sun on my fur. On my skin. I wouldn't want to be faced with that choice the way some of the mates have been."

"Christy?" The little flare of jealousy didn't rise all that high, this time, and Morgan impressed herself with how much her attitude had changed about Matt's former liaison with the woman.

"Nah. She wasn't given a choice. She was dead without Sebastian turning her. Her ex-husband saw to that." Matt frowned, but visibly shook off the dark thoughts. "Some of her friends, though, they had to make a choice. Lissa once told me that if she'd said no to being turned after the accident, Atticus would have let her die...and followed her soon after. She chose life with him, and forsook the sun."

"She loves him," Morgan observed simply. "I know Kelly was willing to die to save Marc when he was poisoned. But he wouldn't have wanted to live without her. I know that for a fact."

"Just as I couldn't live without you, Morgan," Matt said softly, making her heart clench.

He kissed her, and the kiss turned torrid in an instant. Before she knew what was happening, he'd pushed her up against the wall, and she was tearing at his clothes, wanting to feel his flesh against hers. She was wild for him, and it felt like he was just as out of control.

They came together in a sizzling flash of passion, his cock sliding home inside her with little preamble. She felt a faint moment of relief. This was what she wanted. To be possessed by her mate. Fully.

But then, that wasn't enough. She wanted more. She wanted him to take her. To make her come for him. To own her pleasure.

The almost submissive thoughts were strange to her, but they felt right. The female wildcat inside her wanted the male to dominate her—just the tiniest bit. Matt seemed to know just how far to push, how far to assert himself before he pulled back, allowing her to make a few decisions, such as how best to wrap her legs around his waist as he rammed into her repeatedly, almost slamming her willing body against the wall beside the bedroom door.

He nipped at her lips, making her moan, and she wanted more. All he could give. All he could take. She wanted to give him everything—all the love that was inside her—and all the trust they had built between them in the few days they'd been together.

But that's the way it was supposed to be between mates,

her inner cat whispered, then yowled as Matt made them come. Over and over. She cried out and purred at the same time, loving the feel of her mate making violent, blissful, spectacular love to her. As it should be.

"Holy crap, that was intense," she whispered, panting as she began to come down from the most amazing climax.

"I'd tell you two to keep it down, but I know *were*cats in heat aren't to be trifled with."

Morgan swung her head around to meet Cam's gaze through the *open* bedroom door. Her cheeks flamed as she realized the fey knight could see them, but Cam seemed to think nothing of it, merely leaning in to grasp the handle of the door and pull it closed behind him as he left them alone.

Matt chuckled, and Morgan's gaze shot up to his. "Did you know that door was open?"

"Honestly, I didn't know my own name, for a while there. Sorry." Matt didn't look sorry, and Morgan had to admit the situation was kind of funny, even if she had no idea how she would ever face Cam again.

She hid her face against Matt's shoulder. He was still inside her, still pinned up against the wall next to the—now, thankfully, closed—door.

"Don't sweat it, sweetheart," Matt cajoled. "I'm sure Cam's seen a lot in his time. Do you know how *old* that guy is? He talks about time passing in terms of centuries. In all those years, he must've met more than one newly mated couple. And we're shifters. We're not exactly shy about nudity or doing it out in the open."

"Speak for yourself. I was raised by a vampire. An ancient vampire, who lived mostly in the human world. By your standards, I'm sure I'm a prude." She nipped his neck, then raised her head to look into Matt's eyes. "I'm so embarrassed."

Matt kissed her nose. "Don't be. For one thing, you're beautiful. For another, he couldn't see much. Mostly, he probably saw my butt, which I'm pretty sure he's not interested in. I don't think Cam goes both ways, if you know what I mean."

She giggled, as Matt had probably intended. Sure, this incident was embarrassing, but it brought out a bigger issue that had her worried.

"I'm not sure how well I'm going to fit in with your people, Matt. I wasn't raised as a shifter."

"Let's deal with things as they come, Morgan," he counseled, kissing her temple. "I know it's going to be okay, but I know also that you're going to have to see it for yourself." He carried her to the bed, his cock still deep inside her body and regaining its stiffness. "Let's get through tomorrow, and then, we'll deal with the family stuff. Just trust me, it's going to work out. I know it is."

"If you say so," she agreed. Though, as he placed her on the bed and began to move inside her again, her thoughts began to trail away from any possible problems she might have with his family. There were much more enjoyable things to think about, at the moment.

* * *

At dusk that night, the three teams were ready to go. All three mages had been hunted to their locations and watched throughout the day. Irma had gone to work, as usual, and hadn't seemed to notice the magical workings Cam had put in place the night before. Carlos had been at home all day, and the third mage had been traced to his apartment, where Philomena's team had seen him enter around midday, and he hadn't left since.

All was in place.

Marc sent out the take-down order to the other two teams as Atticus sprang the trap in the winery office. For the next half hour, everybody was on the move.

Morgan was at Matt's side, right behind Cam as the fey knight knocked out the magical wardings around Irma's home. Carlos came to the door and tried to fight Cam in a showy magic battle, but Cam was unstoppable. He herded the heavyset man right back into the house, preventing anyone in the quiet, upscale neighborhood from seeing much of anything.

Matt and Morgan followed right behind, securing the door while the *Venifucus* mage and the fey knight continued to battle through the living room and into the kitchen.

Carlos began to get desperate, and things in the room started flying around. Knives came out of the butcher block knife stand and embedded themselves in the wall much too close to Morgan's head for comfort. Ian Sinclair, the vampire enforcer, was searching the rest of the house for surprises while Cam subdued the sorcerer in the kitchen with Morgan and Matt to watch his back.

Carlos threw open a door that led to the basement, and a sulfurous smell assaulted Morgan's nose. A split second later, the most vicious dog she'd ever seen came bounding up the steps, jaws salivating as it launched itself at Cam.

Matt stepped in and wrestled with the beast while Morgan went to help him. When the dog turned to lunge at her, she let her inner cat out to play, swiping at the beast's muzzle with half-shifted claws and screeching at it. The dog seemed to realize it was facing something that wasn't quite human as Matt half-shifted, as well.

The giant dog was dwarfed by Matt's bulky battle form, and its tail lowered, to hide between its legs as it whimpered. Matt maneuvered around to shove the beast back behind the basement door, closing it downstairs while the magic battle moved on toward another door that led to the backyard.

But Cam wasn't letting the sorcerer open another door. And neither was Matt.

He signaled to Morgan, and without words, she knew he wanted her to mirror his movements. They put Cam between them. Matt went to Carlos's left, blocking the door to the backyard, while Morgan took the right. They flanked Cam, moving closer, pinning the mage between the three of them. He had nowhere to go.

But Carlos surprised them, lunging for Morgan, probably

seeing her as the weakest of the three that faced him. She was ready to prove the bastard wrong, though. She let her claws flash and couldn't wait to taste the sorcerer's blood.

Too late, she realized Carlos had reached behind him, into a drawer that held yet more cutlery. She skated too close to the knife in his hand and knew she'd been struck, though it was a shallow cut.

Matt felt his heart clench when he saw Carlos lunge for Morgan. He couldn't let her be hurt—or killed. That was simply unacceptable. He'd rather die if it meant she would live. He loved her that much.

His heart overflowed with love and fear for his mate as he launched himself across the kitchen, onto the sorcerer's back. His claws struck repeatedly, looking for soft flesh. Blood and curses flew as the mage tried one last-ditch attack, but Cam blocked the magic, and Carlos's flesh was no match for half-shifted claws.

One lucky swipe and Carlos was dead, his throat torn beyond repair. For a second, Matt's human side chastised his inner cougar. The cat was glad its enemy was dead, but the man knew they might've gained more from having a prisoner to question than a corpse to bury.

"Pity, that," Cam commented, leaning against the kitchen table, clearly drained from the magical battle that had just taken place. "But it's probably for the best. He was a strong one. It would have been difficult to contain him." Cam straightened from his slouched position. "Which makes me wonder how the rest of our friends are making out."

Ian picked that moment to walk into the room, his gaze lingering on all the blood that had been spilled. But Ian was a mated vampire. His bloodlust was limited to his One now. He was more stable than an unmated bloodletter would have been in a similar situation.

"The rest of the house holds some hidden traps, but nobody else is here. Looks like it was just him and Irma," Ian reported.

"Can you hold the fort here?" Cam asked quickly. "I feel our fellows may need my help."

"We've got this," Matt answered, shifting back to his fully human form.

The half-shifted battle form was painful to hold. Only the strongest Alphas could withstand it for any significant length of time. Matt realized Morgan had held the battle form far longer than any female he'd ever known. Truly, she was his match in every way. She continually impressed the hell out of him.

Cam nodded, and with a blinding whoosh of magic, he simply disappeared.

"Now, that's a neat trick," Matt observed, putting his arm around Morgan's shoulders. "He didn't even have to ask Scotty to beam him up."

* * *

Matt and Morgan began cleaning up what they could of the mess in the kitchen. They didn't want to leave any evidence of what had happened here, and the sooner they began erasing the proof—washing the blood down the drain—the better. Matt also insisted on checking Morgan's little flesh wound. As she'd thought, the cut had been shallow. It was painful, at first, but with her shifter constitution, it had already scabbed over.

They were careful not to venture much farther into the house than they already had. Cameron, or someone with more magic than they had, would probably have to deal with the magical traps Ian had been able to discover.

All in good time. Right now, Morgan was getting antsy to find out how the other teams had made out. It had been agreed in advance that they would call in at a prearranged time, in a specific order, to share their results.

"Almost time," Matt said as he rinsed his hands again in the kitchen sink.

He'd been amazingly casual about wiping down the blood

spatter that had gone all over the kitchen. He'd insisted on Morgan washing off first, while he inspected her cut. Her hands were clean now, though her cat had reveled in the feel of its enemy's blood under its claws.

She hadn't really known she was quite that bloodthirsty, though her cat had always enjoyed hunting and the occasional kill. Morgan hadn't really let her cat kill very often. She figured she was well fed in human form. There was no reason to eat raw food while in her fur. Though she did enjoy chasing birds, rodents and the occasional annoyingly yippy dog, she was more a *catch and release* kind of cat.

Ian rejoined them in the kitchen while Matt hit speed dial on his phone, putting it on speaker so they could all hear and be heard. Lissa answered midway through the first ring. She and the other vampire mates had been left in the make-shift war room, ostensibly to handle communications.

"I've got Marc and Philomena already on the line," Lissa said in a very efficient sort of voice. "Go ahead."

"Carlos is dead," Matt reported quickly.

"So is Irma," Atticus said, satisfaction clear in his tone.

"Ours got away." Philomena sounded really, really pissed off. "Cameron popped in right as we got up to the apartment. There were magical traps all along the way, and we accidentally sprang a few. Hilda's unconscious. She tripped something that knocked her against the wall, and she hit her head. Jeff, Mindy and Prudence are injured too, but not too badly. They're still conscious, though banged up and bleeding a bit. Cam's investigating now and asked us to stay in the entryway. I sent half my team out with the injured, so we don't raise too much attention, but it's a quiet building. Not too many tenants. I don't think anybody's all that interested in us." There was a pause, and she went on, "Cam's coming this way now. He doesn't look pleased. I'm handing him the phone."

Another brief pause and then, Cam's thick brogue came over the line. "I think we underestimated this one. He didn't leave this apartment by any conventional means. He has the ability to transport. That's the only explanation. And the only real explanation for that is that he's not entirely human. I think we've missed the ringleader here, and I'll be damned if I can track him."

"We may not know where he's gone, right now…" Morgan spoke her thoughts aloud. "But we know where he'll be. Eventually."

"The mine." Marc sounded grim. "And he can just transport in without any of us being the wiser."

"We'll have to stake it out," Philomena added. "Round the clock. Every entrance. Every point along the fault. Every vulnerable spot."

"Aye," Cam agreed. "But the one point in our favor is that the kind of magic he needs to do once he gets there canna be rushed. We'll have a narrow window of time during which to stop him." A pause while everyone digested that. "I've nullified the rest of the magical traps here," Cam reported. "He didn't have as many inside the apartment as he had on the way up, and your wolves sprang most of those." His tone was not approving, and Morgan could imagine all those werewolves standing there with their tails figuratively tucked between their legs in shame. "I'm transporting back to Irma's house to finish making it safe for the rest of you to investigate and clean up. Then, I'll pop back to your place, Atticus, if that's all right. We need to start making plans for round-the-clock surveillance."

"By all means, Cam," Atticus spoke up. "You are welcome here, and we value your assistance."

"Yes," Marc agreed. "Thank you for making the way safe for our people. We'll handle the cleanup and bring anything of interest they might find up for discussion as we go along."

"A solid plan," Cam confirmed. "I'm giving the phone back to Philomena."

Philomena came back on the line, and a few more words were exchanged. Marc was conciliatory to the embarrassed Alpha female, and Morgan noticed that Matt made a point to say a few things to make Philomena feel better. It was clear he cared for his Clan and the feelings of those in it.

Any other Alpha might've raked Philomena and her people over the coals for losing such a valuable target and failing in the task set before them, but Matt was understanding and kind. It was clear to Morgan that he knew Philomena already felt bad enough. Yelling at her wouldn't help things. Making her feel valued as part of the Clan, even though she had failed in this mission was more important, right now, and it was exactly what Matt did. Morgan couldn't be prouder of her mate. He was lethal when he needed to be, but he was also one of the most compassionate men she'd ever known.

Cameron appeared in one corner of the kitchen just as the phone call was ending. He conferred quietly with Ian, for a moment, and then, the two of them went off into another part of the house together. Morgan realized they were probably going to work through the magical traps that had been laid throughout the building, which Ian had already scouted earlier.

After Matt ended the call with a promise to clean up here before rendezvousing back at Atticus's home, he turned to Morgan and simply tugged her into his arms. She went willingly. Gratefully. She was a lawyer. She'd never been in a real combat situation like this before. Not really. Hunting prey didn't count because ninety-nine times out of a hundred, she let whatever critter she was after go. Her heart wasn't in the kill. Not the way it had been minutes before.

She'd wanted Carlos dead with a fury that had nearly overwhelmed her. Both the cat and the woman wanted the evil the man represented eradicated from this earth, never to return. The ferocity of her response had surprised her. She hadn't known she really had that kind of rage within her. It was startling. And more than a little scary.

But Matt knew what she needed. She needed him to ground her. To hold her and make her feel like her old self again—even if something had fundamentally changed about her understanding of who and what she really was. Once

Pandora's box was opened, the contents couldn't be stuffed back inside. Morgan would have to deal with the bloodlust she'd felt and the knowledge that she had helped kill a man, albeit a truly evil man, for the rest of her life.

The cat inside her didn't understand her human reticence about taking another's life. Morgan had only let the cat out to play under very controlled circumstances up 'til now. But after tonight, everything would change. The cat was well and truly out of the bag now. It had tasted the freedom to fight and claw, and it would not be denied again.

The human half of her was in agreement, up to a point. Her human side wanted to stop the evil ones. The cat wanted them dead. They had reached a sort of detente where the two would work together and allow Morgan to hold the difficult, half-shifted battle form for as long as she needed it while she fought the bad guys.

"You were magnificent, my love," Matt crooned in her ear, rocking her slightly as he held her tight in his arms. "Your battle form was impressive. And sexy as hell."

"I've never held the shift that long before," she admitted. "I didn't know I could."

He drew back to look into her eyes, and she read approval and pride in his gaze. "You are a true Alpha female, sweetheart. And a formidable one, at that. When you needed your cat's strength, she came, and she didn't fight your human half for dominance. She worked with you. I know how it feels, Morgan." He dipped closer to kiss her lightly. "We are well matched in every way. My cougar admires your strength and power. And you should know I think you're sexy, no matter what form you wear."

She leaned up and kissed him this time, loving the way he made her feel. Accepted. Wanted. Loved.

For the first time in her life, she had found a true home, and it was wherever Matt Redstone was. He was all she would ever need.

CHAPTER THIRTEEN

Matt and Morgan cleaned up the kitchen as best they could. There would be time for a more thorough job later, done by people who specialized in making evidence of supernatural occurrences go away. Matt knew a few such specialists were already in Napa, waiting for a call. He'd be making that call on the drive home, and by morning, nobody would ever be able to tell what had happened here by mundane means.

Which meant any human authorities need never be involved.

Someone would also take care of the mean mutt that was still locked in the basement. Cam had already gone out into the backyard and dismantled some seriously dangerous magic that had been waiting out there, so the outside was safe enough.

Within a half hour, they were back on the road, heading toward Atticus's house. Ten minutes after they arrived, they were in the shower, cleaning off the rest of the blood. Morgan was especially relieved to be able to scrub her hair. Blood had dried in it, and her human side was grossed out by the way her cat side wanted to lick everything clean.

The cat's impulses were stronger than they ever had been before, and Morgan knew she was going to have to spend some time, after all this was over, coming to a new understanding with her wild side. In the meantime, both her inner cat and her human instincts thought it was a really good idea to jump Matt's bones while they shared the big shower in the guest suite.

He hadn't been in here with her before, and the combination of steam, hot water, slippery shampoo and soap, and the sexiest man on Earth was impossible to resist. The shower was plenty big enough for both of them, tiled in a natural stone that made her feel both pampered and as if she was close to nature. The setting appealed to her, but the man appealed even more.

As soon as she'd washed her hair three times to be sure all the dried blood was gone, she turned her attention to her mate. The wildcat inside her, and the woman who wore its human form, wanted him. Now.

She stepped closer to him in the large shower stall. The thing had shower heads all over at different heights and seemed built for two. She put her arms around his waist and slid her wet body against his, reaching up for a kiss.

He obliged her, and then some. Before she knew it, he had her pinned against the stone-tiled wall between two of the largest shower heads. Water continued to rain down around them as steam filled the air.

And then, Matt filled her. There was little foreplay because she needed none. All she wanted was him. Raw. Earthy. Against the wall. Deep within her. Touching her soul and her heart.

Their lovemaking was gritty and harsh but, at the same time, loving and real. Matt pushed her to her limits and beyond, and she loved every second of his possession. He owned her utterly, and she met him thrust for thrust, moan for groan, heartbeat to heartbeat.

Morgan came and then came again before Matt was willing to follow her over the edge into ecstasy. She clenched around his hardness, loving the feel of him within her. His raw power enthralled her, his muscles straining as he fell into completion. She adored the way he let go of his masterful control when he came with her. She cherished the little glimpse of vulnerability in this otherwise potent Alpha. His strength had been almost overwhelming, at first, but now that she knew him—had faced adversity with him—she trusted in his honor and his spirit never to use his power against her.

No, in mating Matt Redstone, she had found a partner she could be proud of and trust utterly. She had also found a protector who, she knew, would go to the ends of the earth to keep her safe. Just as she would for him. He'd been spot on when he said they were well matched.

Her fingernails dug into his shoulders as she rode the final waves of ecstasy. He held her pinned against the wall, his strong body holding her up as if she weighed nothing at all. He trembled slightly as pleasure took him to the stars then returned him to earth, and his forehead rested against hers.

"If you two are done, everybody's waiting for ye," Cam's voice came to them through the bathroom door.

Morgan gasped as Matt lifted his head and chuckled.

"Go away, you old perv," Matt shouted above the rushing of the water, still streaming around them. His tone held amusement, and his words indicated a casual familiarity with the fey warrior she hadn't expected. "We'll be there in a few minutes."

Matt was still deep inside her, and she felt him begin to rise once more. Could they?

He kissed her lightly and withdrew. "Much as I'd love to repeat that, it seems we're being summoned." He held her steady until she had regained her footing. His every move shouted of his care for her, and she felt sort of…cherished. Which was a new experience for her. One she would hug close to her heart for the rest of their lives together… Goddess willing.

"I don't know how I'm going to show my face. Cam keeps finding us making out," she mumbled.

"Doing a bit more than that," Matt added with a chuckle.

"Okay. Screwing like bunnies?" she asked, giving him a

sarcastic smile as she rinsed off, using a bit more soap and quickly taking care of things.

"Hey." Matt caught her attention by cupping her butt and giving her a little squeeze. "At least, this time, we remembered to close the door."

The planning session was in full gear when Matt and Morgan arrived a few minutes later. Their hair was a little damp, but nobody seemed to mind. A new addition had been added to the room since the last time they'd all met here. A massive rolling white board stood off to one side of the room. Drawings and plans of the old mine and the new construction had been taped all over it, most with various colored sticky notes adhered in different locations.

It looked to Morgan like they were dividing up the surveillance duties, and someone had thought to use the sticky notes to color code everything. She walked over to the board while Matt joined the other men at the table, near a bunch of computer screens and telephone hookups. Lissa and Kelly seemed to be the keepers of the sticky notes, so Morgan approached them to learn the code they were using.

Within a few minutes, Morgan had a good grasp of the system they were beginning to work out. She added some suggestions and was able to help the vampire women understand more about the capabilities of the shifter personnel who would be helping with the daytime surveillance. It hadn't been too long ago that both Kelly and Lissa were mortal. They understood sunlight and shadow a little better than some of the male vampires, but they didn't know much about shifters, and that's where Morgan was able to help most.

While the men were busy calling in favors and lining up support, the women were working on deploying the people they already had. It was a fair division of work since it was the males who were older and had more power in the vampire marriages. Each of the brides were only newly made bloodletters and hadn't been around long enough to form the kinds of connections their mates had.

As for Morgan, she had spent most of her life staying away from shifters. Though she understood shifter nature far more than any of the other ladies, she also lacked the kinds of connections Matt had. So, it made sense to parcel out the work that way. They were in a hurry to get coverage on as much of the mine and grounds as they could. All hands were on deck and needed to be used to best advantage.

Before long, they had a workable plan in place, and the men had finished with their phone and video conferences. Morgan saw Marc look over at Kelly, and when she nodded back, it was clear it was time to rejoin the men and compare notes on what they had accomplished. Morgan went to Matt's side, studiously ignoring Cam's raised eyebrow and chuckle.

Marc started the briefing, which he kept short and sweet. Time was of the essence.

"With Matt's help, we managed to get a platoon of Jesse Moore's men en route. They may or may not get here in time to help us, but at least they're on the way. I've also called in a few favors, and we'll have maximum coverage tomorrow night from every member of the Brotherhood within range."

"We've developed a plan for tomorrow," Kelly began, then gestured to Morgan.

"We've broken up the current manpower and grouped them by affiliation and location. We also started identifying points in the mine and the surroundings that could be used for surveillance. We need your input on that." Morgan nodded, spreading the overlay they'd been developing over the topographical map already on the table.

The men crowded around, and everybody went to work, trying to come up with a plan that would provide the most coverage with the few people they had. They moved a few of the spots the women had chosen for various strategic reasons, but for the most part, they had a solid plan within about fifteen minutes.

At that point, they began making phone calls to the werewolves and vampire troops that had come at Marc's command, telling them where to meet and what to look out for. They also took reports and collated information. Matt called some of his people directly and began to make notes, which Morgan helped him organize. The calls took only about five minutes once everyone knew who to call and what to tell them, and then, they began comparing field reports they'd gotten from the people they'd called.

The priestess Hilda was out of the picture, for now. She had a serious concussion and was at the hospital, under observation. Unlike shifters or vamps, human mages could still use regular doctors and medical facilities because their differences from other humans weren't visible to medical science. Magic was something hidden deep within and didn't cause physiological differences that would identify them to human doctors.

"Some of the wolves will be in wolf form," Matt told the group when it was his turn. "It's easier for them to prowl in their fur, and those without two-legged combat training will be much more effective on paws rather than feet. My brother, Steve, and his mate, Trisha, are on their way up here with reinforcements—all trained fighters—but they won't be here for hours, yet."

"For the rest of the night, the Brotherhood will patrol alongside and in cooperation with the shifters," Marc confirmed. "When the sun comes up, it'll all be up to your people, Matt."

Matt nodded. "We can handle it. I'll be positioned in the mine itself. On the fault. If our target gets past all the patrols and sentries at the mine entrances, I'll be the last line of defense."

"And I'll be with you, laddie," Cam said. "I can transport in at the first sign of trouble."

Morgan hadn't known of Matt's plan, but she saw the reason for it. He was the strongest of the shifters present—the highest ranking of the few Alphas on-site. He would have to be posted where there was the most potential for danger.

Morgan didn't want to go back into that deep part of the mine. Hell, she didn't even want to go a foot into any of the surface entrances. But, if Matt was going, she would go with him. No matter what happened, they belonged together now. In danger and in good times.

"We know a bit more about our target from going through his apartment. He didn't leave much behind, but we at least know his name. It's probably an alias, but the name on his lease is Sonny Sidwell," Atticus reported. "A search of records indicates that Mr. Sidwell was born in Georgia fifty-two years ago. Both of his parents are deceased, and he has no other relatives."

"He looks really good for his age," Morgan observed. "He didn't look a day over thirty-five."

"Blood magic can do that. It's an evil business," Cam said, an air of disgust in his tone. "They siphon off their victims' youth along with their blood and take it for themselves. It's possible this Sidwell is much older than the name he is using. Based on the kind of magic he has displayed, to this point, I believe he is at least part fey."

Every eye in the place turned to regard Cameron.

"What makes you say that?" Marc finally asked.

"The ability to transport instantaneously is something very rare among human mages. In fact, I do not know of any in this generation that can wield such power—although I admit I do not know every mage, everywhere. But, in general, strong power calls to me, and I end up meeting or at least observing many of the strong, young human mages before they fully harness their power. I like to keep track of them, in case they stumble too near one of the gateways or otherwise get themselves into trouble before they've gained some control of their abilities."

Cam's voice had taken on a lecturing tone, and Morgan was fascinated by this glimpse into his thoughts.

"It is very likely that Sidwell is an identity this mage has adopted. Probably one of many. I believe bloodletters are familiar with the concept of taking over the identity of someone who died at a young age with no relatives. It can be useful, when trying to exist in this modern world, to blend in by having the proper documentation for birth, social security, driver's license, etc."

Morgan wanted to chuckle at the idea of Cam having a driver's license. For all she knew, he probably did. Though, in all likelihood, it was under some other name. Probably one assumed the way the man using Sonny Sidwell's name had likely assumed that identity.

"So, how much magic do you think we're dealing with here?" Marc asked. "Do you think it's possible that Sidwell could do real damage to the fault all by himself?"

"You'd better believe that, if he can transport, he can cause havoc with that fault," Cam said in a grim tone. "It feels like he needed Irma to get on the property and learn about the construction schedule. I have little doubt, that's why he involved her and her husband in the first place. He probably kept them around because they were strong mages in their own right, but in all likelihood, he doesn't need them to complete the work they'd planned in the mine."

"Then our mission is clear," Matt observed. "We'll just have to cut him off at the pass. Sidwell must not be allowed to do his evil work."

"Agreed," Marc intoned in a voice that sent shivers down Morgan's spine. Sidwell had no idea what kind of fury awaited him if he tried anything in the mine now that they were on guard for him.

* * *

Morgan really, really, *really* didn't want to go back into the mine, but she would go wherever Matt went. She wouldn't wimp out. She was a strong woman. Matt claimed she was an Alpha female. She had to live up to the faith he had put in her.

And it wasn't as if he didn't know how hard this was for her. He took her hand as they walked through the entrance, pausing to look at her.

"If you want to stay up top, I understand." Sweet Mother

of All, he was giving her an out, and she was tempted, for a split second, to take it, but Morgan hadn't gotten where she was by being a wuss. Her mate was going into danger, and she would be at his side—come hell or cave-ins. "Until my brother arrives with the reinforcements, I have to be down there."

"It's okay. Where you go, I go," she promised him.

Well, at least she sounded brave. Now if only she felt that way.

Cameron came toward them, already inside the mine, apparently. He smiled and seemed to let a little of his inner radiance shine through. For a moment, she could've sworn she saw him wearing armor. Glowing armor that made him look invincible.

Then she blinked, and the image faded, but the impression stayed with her. He was a knight, after all. Maybe it wasn't that farfetched to believe he had some kind of glowing, magical armor that she couldn't normally see. And maybe...just maybe...he'd given her a glimpse of it to help shore up her flagging courage.

"I'll be with you too, though you wilna always see me. If you get into trouble like the last time, I swear on my honor that I will get you out." Cam came right up to Morgan and held her gaze. He was dead serious, and she appreciated the solemnity of his vow.

"Thank you," she said, just as seriously. It meant a lot to her that this fey warrior would consider her feelings. She trusted him to help them, should they need it again.

But she trusted Matt more. She knew he would do all in his power to protect her—as she would for him. She might not be the most heavily trained shifter in the world, but *Sensei* Hiro had taught her a thing or two in the past. She could hold her own if it came down to a hand-to-hand fight, and she would fight side-by-side with her mate. He could count on her.

The magical thing was more concerning. They'd been trapped in that other tunnel before, due to magic that caused the very earth to quake. She didn't know what she could do against something like that, which was why it was good to have some seriously heavy magical firepower on their side in the form of the fey knight.

But Cameron couldn't be everywhere at once. He needed the eyes and ears of the shifters and bloodletters to watch and wait. The surveillance net would drop when the enemy was sighted, and an alert would go out to Cameron, wherever he was, to tell him exactly where trouble was brewing.

It was hoped that, between him and the shifters and vampires, they would be able to disable Sidwell. They didn't necessarily want him dead. For one thing, he'd be a good person to interrogate. But they would fight him, and if he died in battle, then so be it. That was the way it had gone for Irma and Carlos. If it went that way for Sidwell too, nobody was going to cry over it.

In fact, Morgan's inner cat wanted to taste Sidwell's blood. Badly. It wanted to slash and claw and eliminate any threat to her mate, and her friends. In that order.

That was new. Before meeting Matt, her friends, and especially Marc, had come first in her loyalty. But throw her new mate into the mix, and he came out on top. Always.

Which felt right. As it should be. As it had been for Marc, when he discovered Kelly. And Atticus, when he had met Lissa. And yes...for Sebastian, when he had finally claimed Christy and learned she was his One.

The fact that Matt had slept with Christy still itched like a burr in Morgan's fur when she thought about it, but slowly, she was coming to terms with it. Seeing Sebastian and Christy together helped. If Sebastian could get past what he'd done— what he'd orchestrated from all accounts—in asking his One to dine on Matt's blood and, inevitably, have sex with him, then Morgan could too. Vamps were just as possessive of their mates as shifters were.

Sebastian had allowed the liaison to make Christy stronger. Matt had explained his reasons, and they made sense too. He'd done it out of a desire to help a woman face her past and her abusive ex-husband. He'd enjoyed it too—of that Morgan had no doubt. Vampires had a certain mojo when they seduced a victim that was said to be the ultimate pleasure. Morgan had never experienced it—and she never wanted to. Nothing could top making love with her mate. Nothing. Not even vampire mojo.

They set off at a brisk pace down the mine shaft, heading for the lowest point in the mine where they had seen the sorcerers at work before. Matt was so freaking proud of Morgan. She was with him, standing by him and overcoming her fears.

He still felt bad about making her come down here, but something inside him said this was where they needed to be. He'd learned to trust his inner voice—his intuition—over the years. Although the others didn't believe it, Matt had the feeling that the showdown with Sidwell was going to happen sooner rather than later.

They didn't have time to waste. And he feared his brother and the cavalry being sent post haste from Las Vegas wouldn't arrive in time. Neither would Jesse Moore's commandos that Marc had hired. This shit was going to go down, and it was going to go down soon. He could feel it, though he prayed he was wrong.

They rounded the curve that would take them to the area where they'd seen the sorcerers before. They moved cautiously, spaced out about ten feet apart in case of an ambush, but none came. When the arrived at the spot where they'd watched from, there was nobody in evidence, though the lights were on.

"Looks like they've got these lights set on a motion sensor system. They came on when we moved into range," Matt observed, pointing to the small device that had been rigged into the old wire on the ceiling from which dangled antique light fixtures every few yards. "The lighting system itself is old, but the sensor is new. High tech."

"For the moment, we are alone," Cam said, looking

around at the area. "Can you show me where they were working and go over what you saw? It might help me learn more about what we're dealing with in terms of magic here."

Matt nodded to Morgan. "Sweetheart, take him over there. I'll stand watch. Just make it quick. We might have company, any time now."

Ideally, he would've liked to have a platoon of his brothers' Green Beret friends at his back, securing the perimeter, but that wasn't meant to be. Not yet. Jesse Moore's special ops group was on the way, but they were still an hour out or more based on the last report. More help was coming up from Vegas, but they were also a couple of hours away. Matt sincerely hoped they got there in time for the party, but the way he was feeling, he didn't think they had that kind of time.

Matt watched as Morgan, efficient as ever, took Cam over to the exact location where they'd seen the *Venifucus* mages at work. He felt some satisfaction knowing that two of the three were no more. They wouldn't be back to stir up the fault and possibly kill millions of people. Good riddance.

Morgan was thorough, but quick, as he'd hoped. His mate had proved over and over to be a smart, feisty, sexy lady, who was perfect for him in just about every way imaginable. The sex was amazing. That went without saying. But he felt a much deeper connection to Morgan than just the physical.

He respected her. He admired her. He couldn't get enough of her—in bed or out. He just wanted to be around her all the time, just to watch her smile or make her laugh. He wanted to spend the rest of his life with her because…he loved her.

Matt had to take a deep breath as that realization finally jelled in his mind. He'd seen how his brothers had reacted to finding their mates, but it really hadn't prepared him for this depth of emotion, this soul-deep connection. He'd never really been so close to a woman before, and now, looking back at the small connection he'd shared with Christy when he witnessed the bond between her and Sebastian, he understood fully, for the first time, everything they'd felt.

He thought he'd known what it was like after seeing the way Sebastian bonded to Christy, but he hadn't expected it would be the same for shifters as it was for bloodletters. Vampires were so…old. Matt figured the fact that those guys had to wait centuries for their One meant they were closer to the edge. More emotional. Or something.

Matt's reasoning had been full of shit. He saw that now. He felt every bit as intensely about Morgan as Sebastian had about Christy. Or as his brothers felt about their mates, for that matter. He realized so much now that he'd been in denial about before.

Then again, he'd never been in love before.

And what a moment to figure it out. If they got out of this alive, Matt was really going to have to work on his timing.

CHAPTER FOURTEEN

Cam and Morgan finished their tour and came back to Matt's position, which wasn't far from where they'd hidden the first time. The design of this excavation had hidden them before, and it would serve the same purpose now. If they could watch from a safe place for Sidwell's arrival, they still might be able to surprise the bastard.

"Did you learn anything?" Matt asked quietly when Cam faced him.

"Quite a bit, actually. If I am right in my deductions, then Sidwell is imperfectly trained in the use of fey magic. It might give me an edge. Then again, it might not. I tend to believe now, after seeing what evidence remains of the work they did here, that Sidwell is only part fey. Probably less than half. Possibly much less. He works mostly in the human magecraft ways, with only small uses of the power of other realms."

"But he can transport. Surely that means he has at least some expertise in fey magic," Morgan asked quietly, ever cautious.

Cam didn't look convinced. "He might be talented in that one regard, but I see no evidence here of a half-fey prodigy."

"Can you really be sure of that?" Matt asked, not willing to underestimate what they might be facing.

"Sure enough to base my strategy on it," Cam assured

them. "I'm afraid, if we see him soon, before reinforcements arrive, I'm going to need you both to distract him while I work the magical attack. Physical attack would be best. Keep him busy while I do my thing. I hate to ask it of you, but I believe that is why you were put here at this time. Both of you." Cam smiled at them, and it held a hint of sadness. "You are newly mated. This should be a time of celebration. Instead, it is probably the most dangerous moment of your existence. I regret that. Deeply. But if we win the day, I will dance at your wedding gladly."

Cam offered his hand, and Matt shook it with a solemn expression. The fey knight then turned to Morgan and caught her in a quick hug.

"Best we get in position now," Cam said briskly, letting Morgan go gently and stepping back. "I'll take the other side. You two arrange yourselves on this side of the work area. Good hunting, my friends."

Matt nodded and took Morgan's hand as Cam walked across the open area to find cover on the other side. She turned toward Matt, and he silenced whatever it was she had been about to say by kissing her quickly.

He'd meant it to be a simple kiss, but he had to tear himself away from her after a few moments, lest he get lost in her. There would be time for that later…if they were successful.

"If Sidwell shows up—and I have to tell you, I really think he will, very shortly—I want you to act as the rear guard. Let me take point, all right?" He felt the urgency of a countdown in his mind. Things were about to happen, and he didn't have time to argue. "Please. Just do it for me, Morgan. I love you."

The declaration seemed to stop any argument she would have made. Thank the Goddess.

"It's about to happen. Don't ask me how I know, but I feel it in my bones. Go over there and hide, Morgan." He let go of her hand with one final squeeze. "You'll be my ace in the hole, okay?"

She walked a step back from him, then stopped. "I love

you too, Matt Redstone. And after this is all over, we're going to have a long talk about your timing."

Matt bit back a laugh, but he couldn't help the smile that split his face. That her thoughts should mirror his own so well shouldn't have surprised him, but it did. He was tickled by the ever-increasing evidence that she was the absolutely perfect match for him in every way.

"I promise we will. Now go, and may the Goddess go with you." He watched as she backed away.

"You too," she said softly before turning to move behind cover.

He watched the spot where she hid and was glad to see that she was invisible to view from all sides. She would be as safe as she could be down here while he and Cam took out the sorcerer. Matt un-holstered his weapons and heard the little snicks and creaks that meant Morgan was doing the same in her hiding place.

They hadn't gone into this unarmed, this time. Matt had taken his own weapons out of the hidden locker in his vehicle and had been surprised by the small arsenal Atticus had put at their disposal. He'd also been surprised by Morgan's choice of weapons. She seemed to favor blades, though he had been glad to see she'd also chosen a 9mm handgun that she handled with familiar caution.

She knew how to shoot. Marc had assured him of that privately. Marc, her surrogate father and part-time brother figure, had made sure she'd had self-defense and weapons training. Thank the Goddess.

The itch at the back of Matt's neck began to drive him absolutely nuts, and then, it happened. Between one breath and the next, Sidwell appeared in the center of the open area.

He blinked for a moment, apparently suspicious of the lights already being on before his arrival. *Shit.*

"Who's there?" Sidwell demanded in a firm voice, even while he spread his fingers and opened his hands at his sides, gathering energy. Even Matt could feel the sizzle in the air and see the fire in the man's palms as he prepared for a confrontation.

Wait a minute. Fire?

Sure enough, when Matt looked again, there were actual flames in the man's hands. Though he'd never seen such a thing before, Matt had heard the stories about different kinds of magic users who held power over different elements. His new sister-in-law, Trisha, who was part water sprite, could manipulate water to do pretty much anything she wanted it to do. She had told him about the differences between elemental beings, like herself and her family, and magic users who could manipulate certain elements.

It looked for all the world like Sidwell was one of those sorcerers who could call fire. Matt thought about it, for a moment, and realized that, while formidable, in a way, they were lucky that there wasn't much down here that could burn.

Matt tried to think fast. Fire needed oxygen to burn. There were, however, a sufficient number of air shafts, and a system that allowed for the conveyance of fresh air even into the deepest parts of the old mine. So, while there was no danger of suffocation, it also meant that the mage's fire could still burn.

"Show yourself," Sidwell demanded, turning in a slow circle to look all around the open area.

This section of the mine had been a collection and work area, which was in their favor. There was a large open spot in the center with dug-out connecting caverns. Big pillars of rock had been left standing to support the ceiling that were concave on either end and thick enough around the middle to comfortably hid behind.

The lights had only been strung in the main corridor, so the side caverns of varying sizes were filled with deep shadows. The dark meant little to shifter sight, but it was pretty clear Sidwell was having trouble seeing into the darkness. He squinted and squirmed before an idea seemed to come to him.

With a sudden whoosh, he lobbed a fireball against the far

wall of the nearest cavern to him. It lit the area, burning for a few seconds against the far wall of rock, allowing Sidwell to see into the chamber. It was empty.

Sidwell turned and repeated the move with the next chamber, firing more quickly now, lighting up each cavern around him. Matt hid behind a rough-hewn stone pillar, confident that his comrades were doing the same. With any luck, Sidwell wouldn't spot any of them, and nobody would get singed.

But luck wasn't with them. Matt's heart practically stopped when he heard Morgan cry out. He held his breath when he saw her come out from behind the pillar she'd been hiding behind, tendrils of flame wrapping around, but not quite touching, her body. The flames moved forward, and she had to move with them or be burned.

Neat trick. But it sucked. Morgan was out in the open, her hands held up, her weapons nowhere in evidence. *Good girl*, Matt thought.

"You're the lawyer, right?" Sidwell asked as Morgan moved closer, his flames making her move out of hiding and into the open area. "Carlos warned me about you. Said you were too nosey for your own good. And too loyal to the bloodsucker who raised you. How did that work, exactly? He fucked you and fed on you, but never turned you?" Sidwell coaxed her closer, gesturing with his fingers to reinforce the flame's hold on her. "Sucks to be you, doesn't it? But I don't get why you're still here, now that he's got some other whore and she's sucking his blood too."

Though Sidwell prodded her, Morgan kept silent. Matt was glad. Anything she said could set this guy off, and she was doing just what Cam had asked for—albeit not quite the way they had planned. She was distracting the sorcerer while Cam did his own magic. The longer Sidwell kept talking, playing with Morgan—though Matt was going to step in shortly to take the sorcerer's focus off his mate—the better for Cam and his spell crafting.

"Well? What have you got to say before I fry you?" Sidwell

prodded. If ever there was a time to speak, this was it, and Morgan didn't disappoint as Matt maneuvered around in the shadows, repositioning himself to best advantage.

As it was, Morgan was in his line of fire. He had to move, to make things safer for her. Not that being wreathed in live flames was what anyone would call *safe*.

"I'm surprised, Mr. Sidwell," Morgan began. Her voice held just the right amount of panic and knowledge. As long as she remained interesting, Sidwell wouldn't hurt her. Or so Matt believed. "Your intel seems to be flawed. Or didn't you know I was Marc's pet shifter?"

"A shifter? Raised among vampires?" Sidwell looked truly surprised. And distracted. Score one for their side. "I don't believe it. They would've sucked you dry to get a hit off your blood."

"Actually, no. None of the Brotherhood has ever bitten me. As Marc's ward, I was considered off limits."

"Astonishing," Sidwell commented, still drawing her closer. She was about halfway into the open area now. Matt wouldn't let her get much closer to the sorcerer, but he was looking for the perfect opening. "But I suppose some of those bloodsuckers are old fashioned and old enough to be eccentric. So, tell me, what sort of animal are you?"

"Now, that would be telling," Morgan said, crying out when one of the streamers of flame reached up to touch her shoulder, burning through her shirt and causing a red welt to rise on her skin.

Oh, Sidwell was going to pay for that one. Matt was going to slice the bastard into little ribbons with his claws. Slowly.

"Tut, tut, Ms. Chase. I asked nicely. If you prefer not to play, I can always incinerate you, now rather than later."

"I'm a cat," she spit out, fear and anger mixing in her voice. "A panther."

Sidwell seemed to consider her. "I guess I can see that. You've got the hair and the eyes. Not to mention the body. You're not the first shapeshifter I've met. Nor the first I've killed."

"Oh, really? Who else did you kill? Anybody I know?" Morgan was doing her job, keeping him talking.

"Not unless you've been to Las Vegas lately. There was some action down there a while back that I got to help out with. But they were wolves, I think. Mongrels, really."

"Ray Fesan?" Morgan connected the dots to come up with an astonishing conclusion. Matt hadn't realized this mage might be connected to what went down in his hometown. "I heard a werewolf named Ray Fesan was killed in Las Vegas."

Sidwell bowed his head mockingly. "You are very well informed. Yes, I believe that was his name. He was just one of many that I have killed over the centuries. And I will kill many more of your kind. And all the Others. Vampires, mages who refuse to see the truth. Everyone who stands against me will die."

The sorcerer was working up to a good head of steam, and the fire around Morgan was flaring. It was time to act. Matt stepped into the light.

"Let her go." Matt's assault rifle was aimed at the sorcerer's heart.

It wasn't his only weapon, but it would do, for now. Guns had a way of distracting people—even sorcerers.

Matt was prepared for what he figured would come next. A lick of flame lashed out at him from the mage, wrapping around and heating the barrel. Matt had removed the ammo from it the moment he realized flames were the sorcerer's primary weapon. No exploding bullets would go off in his face, but Sidwell didn't know that. Not yet, anyway.

Matt threw the empty weapon toward Sidwell and opened fire with a handgun he'd kept ready, catching the sorcerer off guard enough that the flames unwrapped from around Morgan. Sidwell called them back to protect himself. The moment he surrounded himself in a wall of flame, taking back all his tendrils, Morgan leapt clear.

Matt was on his right; Morgan had leapt to the left. She commenced firing with the handgun she'd had hidden in her waistband, behind her back, while Matt reloaded. By keeping up the barrage of bullets, they forced Sidwell to keep his shield of flames around himself. While he was doing that, it seemed like he couldn't go on the offense, which was exactly what they needed, right now. They had to keep the status quo until Cam was ready with his spell, but it was going to have to be soon. They couldn't keep this up forever. Eventually, they'd run out of bullets, or Sidwell would try a new tactic.

"Anytime now," Matt muttered, hoping Cam would hear.

Matt wasn't sure if Sidwell could hear anything behind the wall of flame he'd erected between himself and the bullets, but Matt wasn't taking any chances. Cam would show himself when he was good and ready. Matt just prayed it would be soon.

Morgan moved slightly, apparently looking for a better angle, which caused Sidewell's flame wall to flicker. Or maybe it was something Cam had done, but whatever the cause, one of Matt's bullets got through. And then another. And another.

They weren't inflicting any major damage on the sorcerer. The flames were taking a lot of the oomph out of the rounds, slowing them enough that they didn't really penetrate Sidwell's skin, but they were hitting, and that was something that hadn't happened before. The flame wall was becoming more transparent, and Matt could see the panic on Sidwell's face.

That's when Matt knew Cameron was definitely in the act. Sidwell seemed to realize it too. He whirled to face Cam, who had come out from behind a stone pillar. He was glowing with the fey energy that made it appear as if he was wearing translucent, golden armor.

It was quite an imposing sight, but Matt couldn't afford distraction now. He still had to help Cam stop Sidwell. Matt wouldn't rest easy until Sidwell was under their total control. Or dead. Dead was good too. At least as far as Sidwell was concerned.

Matt moved closer to the sorcerer, creeping up behind him. He noticed Morgan approaching from the other side, a little more cautiously. Matt would've waved her back, but he knew they needed three points to their pincer. Cam was in front, facing the enemy dead on. Matt and Morgan were there to keep Sidwell from retreating.

At least, that was the theory.

Instead of diminishing, Sidwell's flames grew brighter, all of a sudden. Cam advanced, and Matt didn't hold back. No matter what happened, Sidwell had to be stopped, and this was their one and only chance to do it.

As that thought occurred, Matt finally noticed the circle in the dirt. Cam must've done it earlier, and it looked like the fey knight was herding the sorcerer into the circle he'd scratched out. There wasn't time to question. Matt knew circles were significant in magic. He half-shifted into his battle form and roared, forcing the sorcerer back and to the left a little.

He didn't dare look at the floor. Not while Sidwell was eyeing him. Cam was waving his hands around in arcane symbols, and the sorcerer was forced to move again. Morgan, in her battle form, joined in, forcing another move. Then, just an inch more to the right and...there.

Sidwell was in the circle, and Cam let loose with his magic, trapping the sorcerer within the circle he'd surreptitiously cast. Cam came forward, and battle was engaged.

Sidwell threw everything he had at the circle that caged him. Flames roared within the circle in a dome of protection Cam was holding. Or, at least, that's how Matt interpreted what he was seeing. Cam was sweating, and his hands were shaking as his fingers twisting into those arcane glyphs that Matt had seen used only a few times by high-powered magic users.

Cam's arms were trembling, and his whole body shook with the force of the power being thrown against his circle. The flames flared higher and higher, the cavern heating even though the flames were well contained. For now.

"Run!" Cam shouted at them. "I can't hold him much longer. He's going to flame out, and when he does, there will be an explosion. You two need to be out of the tunnels before then—and get everyone else clear of the tunnel system. I don't know how far his flames will go."

"What about you?" Morgan yelled over the fury of the crackling, snapping, sparkling energy zooming around the cavern and bouncing off the rock walls.

"I can transport. You can't. Get out now, while you still can!" Cam shouted back. The sound was getting louder as the power ramped up another notch.

Matt didn't need to hear any more. He grabbed Morgan's hand, and they ran as they had once before—this time through a different, wider tunnel. He was still in his battle form, but Morgan had shifted back to human, her clothing stretched out of shape a bit but still on her body. She had pulled out her cell phone as she ran, hitting the speed-dial signal they had set up as a fail-safe. With any luck, the call would get everyone who was near the mine moving away.

Cam had insisted on this contingency, and only now, did Matt truly appreciate the effort it had taken to get every cell phone on every member of the team set up. If the Goddess was smiling on them, the fail safe would work, and everybody would turn tail and run. Matt had a feeling when the magic battle below ground finally hit the boiling point, the fault was going to be the least of their immediate worries.

Matt ran, but Morgan was slower in her human form. The same intuition that had made him believe the confrontation was going to happen before the cavalry could arrive told him now, that they didn't have much time left before the sorcerer flamed out, as Cam had called it. He swooped down and picked up Morgan around her waist, running full out in his half-shifted form, leaping over vast distances, eating up the yards of the tunnel, straining toward the surface.

And then, the earth trembled, and a booming roar came from deep within the mine.

They were almost to the entrance. Matt could see the wide opening that promised safety and fresh air. They were almost there…but would they make it?

Morgan turned her head into his neck as the fire caught up

with them, for a split second, before they burst into the open air. Matt lunged to the side, out of the stream of intense fire that lasted for minutes rather than seconds.

He panted, stumbling away from the pulsating flames with Morgan still held tight against his chest. He felt raw in places and could smell singed fur, but they were alive. That had to count for something.

"Are you okay, sweetheart?" he asked, setting her down on a smooth, flat rock, some distance from the dying flames.

"I'm fine. How about you? I think your hair melted a bit in spots." She reached up to touch his hair. "Oh, Matt. Does anything hurt? Were you burned anywhere?"

"I don't think so," he assured her. "I feel okay. Just a little crispy, but not too badly singed, thank the Goddess."

He sat next to her, both of them watching the showy fire that was only just starting to burn itself out.

"I hope everybody else got away in time," Morgan murmured, looping her arm around his waist and leaning her head against his shoulder.

"I hope Cam did too," Matt agreed. "He did a heck of thing down there."

"So did you two." Cam's voice came from behind them.

Matt stood and whirled to face the fey knight. He looked a little worse for wear, but he was alive and whole. Like Matt, a little singed but okay. And he looked like he was barely staying on his feet.

Morgan got up and guided Cam to the rock they had been sitting on, urging him to rest.

"Are you all right?" she asked, fussing over the knight.

"Is Sidwell gone?" Matt was more concerned about their enemy, at the moment. He needed to know if he still had to be on guard for attack from the fire mage.

"Sidwell did, indeed, flame out quite spectacularly. There is nothing left but a pile of ash where he once stood. When the priestess is fit to work again, she can take care of his remains. For now, the threat is over. Sidwell is no more."

"Thank the Goddess for that," Morgan said, leaning

against the rock, next to Cam.

"Aye, lassie. You can say that again," was Cam's wry comment.

* * *

Morgan was once again taking a shower in the luxurious shower attached to Atticus and Lissa's guest room. She'd spent more time getting clean...among other things...in this room over the past couple of days than usual. Then again, it had been a very messy few days—both figuratively and literally.

Cameron had left them at the gold mine, declaring that he would go to his home Underhill in order to recoup his spent energy. He'd looked old and haggard after the magic battle with Sidwell, and in urgent need of rest. Morgan had insisted on seeing him safely to the portal, though it had meant going back into the very tunnel that had collapsed around them before.

But Cam was weary, and she could at least do that for him. She worried about whether he'd be okay on the other end, but he assured her that he had friends there too, who would help him if need be. She and Matt had watched him go through the portal, and for just a split second, the scent of unearthly flowers and a warm breeze lifted her hair. She thought she could see a green meadow and an honest-to-goodness castle in the distance on the other side of the hazy barrier, but as soon as Cam walked through, the portal collapsed, and they were left looking at a wall of scorched rock.

Every tunnel had been charred by the mage's explosion. The old lighting system was toast, but so was anything the bad guys had put in down here, which was a boon. The werewolves would rebuild the parts of the infrastructure they wanted, and they had a clean slate, so to speak, on which to work...even if it was a bit sooty.

Matt stepped into the shower, and her thoughts went

immediately to his burns.

"How are you feeling? Let me see your backside," she demanded. Her tone was filled with worry, but Matt's arched eyebrow made her think of other things.

"Now that's what I like to hear," Matt teased, but turned around so she could inspect his skin.

He was a little bruised in places, but the worst of the injuries were already healing, leaving only the red marks behind. His shifter constitution meant that even those marks would be gone in a few hours. Thank goodness.

"I'm relieved. You took the brunt of that blast of flame." She stepped into his arms and rubbed her wet body against his, her feline side wanting to snuggle for reassurance.

"The burns are mostly gone, as you saw, but I don't know what I'm going to do about my hair." He reached up and ran his fingers through the scraggly, uneven locks that had been charred by the flame, just on one side.

"Buzz cut?" She offered, smiling. "Just until it grows back."

"Yeah, I guess I'll have to, but my brothers are going to tease the shit out of me for it." He rubbed his hair, one last time, then brought his hand down to curve around her waist.

"Be glad you're around to tease," she reminded him. "That was a little too close for comfort."

"Way too close," he agreed, bending down to kiss her lips. "Let's not do anything like this again for a century or so, okay?"

She smiled up at him as he moved them both under the spray of multiple shower heads.

"I'm totally fine with that."

And she was totally fine with the way he made love to her. Over and over again.

* * *

The very next evening, the Brotherhood threw a grand party at the vineyard office, which had been studiously examined by the local priestess. Hers was the second magical check because Cameron had already dismantled Irma's wards even before they went after her. But it was better to be safe than sorry, and the priestess blessed the building and grounds anew.

The bash was to celebrate several things. The arrival of the cavalry, finally, from both Las Vegas and Moore's men from Wyoming was one of them. It was a rare opportunity for the two groups to mix and mingle, which wasn't common in shifter circles. Once a shifter settled in a territory, they usually didn't leave it too often.

They were also celebrating the end of another *Venifucus* threat, which was something to truly be thankful for. The Brotherhood also wanted to formally welcome the werewolf Pack and others who would be living in the development to Napa. But the biggest cause for celebration, as far as Matt was concerned, was his mating with Morgan.

The Brotherhood had surprised them with generous wedding presents, and Marc had made a big fuss about giving Morgan's care and safety into Matt's keeping. The Brotherhood had also welcomed Matt as an honorary member since he was marrying in, so to speak.

And the shifters had brought small gifts and their sincere good wishes to the couple. Every true mating was something to be celebrated in grand style, and this would probably be the first of several parties held in their honor. Matt knew for a fact that his brothers would be throwing a bash when he brought Morgan home to Las Vegas to meet the rest of the Clan, and he was looking forward to it, even if she was a little intimidated by the idea.

Morgan still wasn't completely comfortable around shifters. That much was obvious. But she was making an effort. For him. Which made him feel about ten feet tall.

He would do anything for her. He loved her deeply and truly...and forever.

Matt leaned down to kiss her, and she responded in kind, cupping his jaw with her soft hand. He loved her touch.

Almost as much as he loved her.

Matt had traveled many roads and done a lot in his life, but nothing would ever outshine this moment. They were among friends, celebrating a victory over evil and the never-ending cycle of life…and love.

Life couldn't get much sweeter than it was right now.

"What?" Morgan asked, smiling up at him from only inches away as he stared into her eyes.

"I love you, Morgan," he answered simply. That tiny, little, powerful phrase really covered it all.

"And I love you, Matt Redstone."

EPILOGUE

As the lava flowed in a volatile mountain range thousands of miles away from the party in Napa Valley, a rift opened between the many realms, and a small woman walked through. Her robes caught fire in the heat of the volcano's inner chamber.

Surrounded in flame, Elspeth came back to the mortal realm.

The Destroyer had returned.

# # #

ABOUT THE AUTHOR

Bianca D'Arc has run a laboratory, climbed the corporate ladder in the shark-infested streets of lower Manhattan, studied and taught martial arts, and earned the right to put a whole bunch of letters after her name, but she's always enjoyed writing more than any of her other pursuits. She grew up and still lives on Long Island, where she keeps busy with an extensive garden, several aquariums full of very demanding fish, and writing her favorite genres of paranormal, fantasy and sci-fi romance.

Bianca loves to hear from readers and can be reached through Twitter (@BiancaDArc), Facebook (BiancaDArcAuthor) or through the various links on her website.

WELCOME TO THE D'ARC SIDE…
WWW.BIANCADARC.COM

OTHER BOOKS BY BIANCA D'ARC

Brotherhood of Blood
One & Only
Rare Vintage
Phantom Desires
Sweeter Than Wine
Forever Valentine
Wolf Hills
Wolf Quest

Tales of the Were
Lords of the Were
Inferno

Tales of the Were – The Others
Rocky
Slade

Tales of the Were – Redstone Clan
The Purrfect Stranger
Grif
Red
Magnus
Bobcat
Matt

String of Fate
Cat's Cradle
King's Throne
Jacob's Ladder
Her Warriors

Guardians of the Dark
Half Past Dead
Once Bitten, Twice Dead
A Darker Shade of Dead
The Beast Within
Dead Alert

Dragon Knights
Maiden Flight
The Dragon Healer
Border Lair
Master at Arms
The Ice Dragon
Prince of Spies
Wings of Change
FireDrake
Dragon Storm
Keeper of the Flame
Hidden Dragons

Resonance Mates
Hara's Legacy
Davin's Quest
Jaci's Experiment
Grady's Awakening
Harry's Sacrifice

Jit'Suku Chronicles
Arcana: King of Swords
Arcana: King of Cups
Arcana: King of Clubs
Arcana: King of Stars
End of the Line

StarLords
Hidden Talent
Talent For Trouble
Shy Talent

Gifts of the Ancients
Warrior's Heart

Grizzly Cove
All About the Bear

TALES OF THE WERE ~ THE OTHERS
ROCKY

On the run from her husband's killers, there is only one man who can help her now... her Rock.

Maggie is on the run from those who killed her husband nine months ago. She knows the only one who can help her is Rocco, a grizzly shifter she knew in her youth. She arrives on his doorstep in labor with twins. Magical, shapeshifting, bear cub twins destined to lead the next generation of werecreatures in North America.

Rocky is devastated by the news of his Clan brother's death, but he cannot deny the attraction that has never waned for the small human woman who stole his heart a long time ago. Rocky absented himself from her life when she chose to marry his childhood friend, but the years haven't changed the way he feels for her.

And now there are two young lives to protect. Rocky will do everything in his power to end the threat to the small family and claim them for himself. He knows he is the perfect Alpha to teach the cubs as they grow into their power... if their mother will let him love her as he has always longed to do.

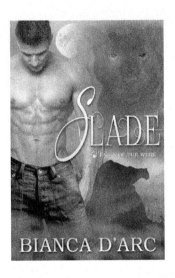

TALES OF THE WERE ~ THE OTHERS
SLADE

The fate of all shifters rests on his broad shoulders, but all he can think of is her.

Slade is a warrior and spy sent to Nevada to track a brutal murderer before the existence of all shifters is revealed to a world not ready to know.

Kate is a priestess serving the large community of shifters that have gathered around the Redstone cougars. When their matriarch is murdered and the scene polluted by dark magic, she knows she must help the enigmatic man sent to track the killer.

Together, Slade and Kate find not one but two evil mages that they alone can neutralize. Slade finds it hard to keep his hands off his sexy new partner, the cougars are out for blood, and the killers have an even more sinister plan in mind.

Can Kate somehow keep her hands to herself when the most attractive man she's ever met makes her want to throw caution to the wind? And can Slade do his job and save the situation when he's finally found a woman who can make him purr?

Warning: Contains a tiny bit of sexy ménage action with two smokin' hot men..

TALES OF THE WERE ~ REDSTONE CLAN 1
GRIF

Griffon Redstone is the eldest of five brothers and the leader of one of the most influential shifter Clans in North America. He seeks solace in the mountains, away from the horrific events of the past months, for both himself and his young sister. The deaths of their older sister and mother have hit them both very hard.

Lindsey Tate is human, but very aware of the werewolf Pack that lives near her grandfather's old cabin. She's come to right a wrong her grandfather committed against the Pack and salvage what's left of her family's honor—if the wolves will let her. Mostly, they seem intent on running her out of town on a rail.

But the golden haired stranger, Grif, comes to her rescue more than once. He stands up for her against the wolf Pack and then helps her fix the old generator at the cabin. When she performs a ceremony she expects will end in her death, the shifter deity has other ideas. Thrown together by fate, neither of them can deny their deep attraction, but will an old enemy tear them apart?

Warning: Frisky cats get up to all sorts of naughtiness, including a frenzy-induced multi-partner situation that might be a little intense for some readers.

TALES OF THE WERE ~ REDSTONE CLAN 2
RED

A water nymph and a werecougar meet in a bar fight... No joke.

Steve Redstone agrees to keep an eye on his friend's little sister while she's partying in Las Vegas. He's happy to do the favor for an old Army buddy. What he doesn't expect is the wild woman who heats his blood and attracts too much attention from Others in the area.

Steve ends up defending her honor, breaking his cover and seducing the woman all within hours of meeting her, but he's helpless to resist her. She is his mate and that startling fact is going to open up a whole can of worms with her, her brother and the rest of the Redstone Clan.

TALES OF THE WERE ~ REDSTONE CLAN 3
MAGNUS

A tortured vampire, a lonely shifter, and a deadly power struggle of supernatural proportions. Can their forbidden love prevail?

Magnus is the quiet brother. The one who keeps to himself. But he has good reason for his loner status. Two years ago, he met a woman. Not just any woman. This woman made his inner cougar stand up and roar. Even in human form, he purred when she stroked him, a sure sign that she was his mate. And mating is a very serious thing among shifters. Too bad the lady had fangs...

Mag discovers Miranda being held captive. She's been tortured to the point of -madness. Mag frees her and takes her to his home, nursing her back to health and defying all convention to keep her with him. He doesn't ever want to let her go again, but he knows the deck is stacked against them.

When a vampire uprising threatens, Mag and Miranda are in the middle. More than just their necks are on the line when a group of vampires seek to kill them and overthrow the current Master. But they have powerful allies, and their renewed relationship has made both of them stronger than either would ever be alone.

Can they stay together forever? Or will the daylight—and their two very different worlds—tear them apart again?

WWW.BIANCADARC.COM

CPSIA information can be obtained at www.ICGtesting.com
Printed in the USA
LVOW04s1835020915

452548LV00018B/875/P

9 781514 695203